ALMOND, QUARTZ, AND FINCH

Lisa Bunker

New Wind Publishing
Sacramento, California

New Wind Publishing
Copyright © 2023 by Lisa Bunker.

Library of Congress Control Number: 2023907481

ISBN 978-1-929777-31-0 (paperback)
ISBN 978-1-929777-32-7 (ebook)
ISBN 978-1-929777-33-4 (audiobook)

Cover illustration by Cygnus Madrose
Cover design by Karen Phillips

Almond, Quartz, and Finch / Lisa Bunker. -- 1st ed.

New Wind Publishing
Sacramento, California 95819
www.newwindpublishing.com

Praise for *Almond, Quartz, and Finch*

A compelling fantasy with important themes...the writing is beautiful, the characters are well-developed and believable. This book, along with an earlier stellar novel, *Zenobia July*, firmly places Bunker as a premier writer for the LGBTQ+ community.
—**San Francisco Book Review**

Unlike any coming of age story I've read before, full of intricate world building, adventure, and gender defying characters. This is a life affirming book that many people—young and old—will find magic, belonging, and solace in; a tale about growing up, trusting in your community, and being brave enough to live exactly as you are.
— **Mariama J. Lockington**
Stonewall Honor-winning author of *In the Key of Us*

In this imaginative and fiercely hopeful tale about family, friendship, and freedom, Bunker articulates how deeply we know our true genders, and how important it is to honor that knowledge.
— **Misa Sugiura**
author of *Momo Arashima Steals the Sword of the Wind*

A well-told and exciting YA fantasy, both gender-affirming and a realistic look at friends coming of age in turbulent times.
— **Susan Schafer**
The Book Shoppe, Inc.

From start to finish, a book I couldn't put down. The perfect balance of action and intrigue, along with a groundbreaking exploration of gender identity. Lush prose, relatable characters, and a nuanced world are hallmarks of this beautiful, important novel, which is sure to resonate with a wide spectrum of readers.
— **A. J. Sass**
award-winning author of *Ellen Outside the Lines*

Bunker creates a rich world that feels lived in and full—one that allows for a nuanced and fresh exploration of gender. Fascinating and dazzling, it is a rare pleasure to follow this journey.

— **Caroline Huntoon**
author of *Skating on Mars*

For Dawn, my precious One.

My heart is yours forever.

Chapter 1

LONG AGO in the forgotten land of Irzem, a parched and sweltering fiefdom, refugees from another forgotten land, the northern realm of Nezel, labored as little more than slaves. They had fled their homeland after zealots from among their countrymen had overthrown and murdered their leader Meb Netál, visionary founder of the Way. Following reports that trickled back from the first few to leave, family after family headed south in search of even the least sense of safety and hope. This was how, in time, a dozen dozen or so Nezel immigrants found themselves toiling as servants in a dusty little castle in an arid wasteland, under the rule of a people who did not look, act, speak, believe, or worship as they did.

On a certain summer morning through the furnace air came young Nemtori, flitting like a trick of the eye along the base of the fortress wall. In the Nezel tongue, Nemtori means "Almond." Such were the child-names Nezel parents who followed the Way gave their children: simple words from daily life, providing no hint of girl or boy. Almond's feet made no sound on the hot earth, and the homespun breechclout and tunic all Nezel youth wear until their Namings flapped around the servant's slight frame. Still, one watching would not say, "Here is a frail creature." Wire bent by an alert and agile mind danced under that thin wool. Eyes deep in watchfulness sparked in that thin face.

Rounding a corner, Almond came face to face with Felshad, which in Nezel means "Quartz." Almond and Quartz were as close as could be to siblings without sharing blood. Felshad's birth parents were gone, one dead, one long ago fled. In their absence he had been raised as much by Almond's mother and father as by anyone.

Quartz greeted Almond with a grin. "Woolworks again today?"

Almond nodded.

"I am supposed to sweep in their temple, as usual, but listen, Lork has the charge." Lork was one the Irzemi overseers, a small prim man with an air of detached heartlessness, known for imposing severe punishment for the least error. "So, what say you? A good morning for one of your hiding-holes?"

Almond, an intensely private young soul, had over time developed a collection of secret places around the castle, suitable either for solitude, when that was what veir tender willow spirit craved, or for the craft of spying, for vo took a lively pleasure in watching others without being seen veirself. As a rule vo preferred to undertake such sojourns alone, but occasionally vo did take comfort in Quartz's rough energy, especially in troubled times, and these were troubled times. Both in the fortress as a whole, and at home in the Nez family hut, strife loomed.

Almond nodded again, agreeing to Quartz's plan. "The deep stores, perhaps?" vo said in veir soft voice.

"That would do. Maybe we can find an open basket of pistachios."

Into the servants' gate they slipped, scattering foraging fowl, nodding at the drowsing guard, who twitched an eyelid in reply. They passed the ornamented archway that led to the luxurious quarters of the noble family, then the plainer openings leading to kitchen, woolworks, stores, laundry. They continued on within the circuit of the fortress wall, along the edges of the orchard and a garden, and down a long cloister toward a certain sluice, pointless now in the dry season. It would serve its intended purpose half the year round, when the rains came. Meanwhile it allowed entry to one of the most secret hiding places Almond knew.

Chapter 2

A FEW BODY-LENGTHS down the sluice, a fissure in the wall opened into one of the natural crevices that riddled the stone under the citadel. This crack twisted sideways, then dropped into utter darkness. Almond kept a candle stub and flint and tinder in a pocket, considering them essential tools for exploring caves or lurking behind walls, but vo did not bring these items out on this occasion. Vo knew veir way by touch, by the taste of the dust in the air, by the hushing of air past the tiny hairs on veir skin.

Down the two squeezed, Almond in silence, Quartz growling now and then as he maneuvered the narrower places. His gonehand did not hinder him, but his size did. Soon he would grow too large to make this journey. At length a faint silhouette of rock in front of rock showed beneath their feet, and the crevice widened until it opened into the darkest reaches of a dimly lit stone chamber.

They had entered the fortress's deepest, and therefore coolest, storeroom, a natural cavern discovered long ago by the builders and made useful by the widening of the entrance and the mounting of a door. Sacks of millet, jars of olives, baskets of fruit, strings of dried fish, and other provender crowded the space. The smells of the stores mingled with the sour-clay whiff of the rock around them. The dim illumination came from a single small tunnel-skylight bored through thick stone. As they entered, mice skittered in the gloomier reaches, then fell quiet.

Almond settled into veir favorite spot, a smooth natural hollow in the stone behind a tall rank of millet-sacks. Gaps between the laden bags allowed glimpses of an edge of this and a curve of that in the main part of the chamber. Vo curled veir body into the cupped hands of the rock, feeling the sweet lifting of the weight vo had carried all this day, for many days.

Quartz slipped out among the stores long enough to filch a handful of pistachios from a basket. On his return he plumped down cross-legged beside Almond and held out the nuts, offering half. Almond shook veir head. Crunching shells open with his teeth, Quartz took up the thread of a running grievance. "How much longer must we wait?"

Almond did not answer.

"I've been ready for the Naming since forever." Having reached their thirteenth summers, both Felshad and Nemtori were deemed ready for the rite of Naming, when, according to the dictates of the Way, they would choose their paths forward into the rest of their lives, whether as woman, man, or in between, as well as the names they would carry along those paths.

Still no answer, but the absence spoke of no want of words between them. Quartz was used to Almond's silences.

Quartz began tossing pistachio shells over the rank of sacks. They clicked and clattered in the cave beyond. "And now because a stupid old woman is dying, we have to wait even longer!" He meant Omdyun Z'Borforeh, the Irzemi ruler of the fortress and the arid lands round about. The Lady Omdyun was ancient and had long been failing. She lay near death in a chamber in the highest tower, and many aspects of castle life—including the Nezel Naming ritual—were altered or postponed.

"Cerach," said Almond. "Cerach."

At the sound of his already long-ago chosen man-name, Quartz's quick ire drained away, though the crease remained between his eyes. "Yes. But I want everyone to say it, not just you."

"Soon," Almond said. Veir thin hand found Quartz's arm above the severed place, squeezed a moment, withdrew.

"What about you? Have you chosen?"

Almond's mouth went hard, veir eyes elusive.

"Have you?"

Almond did not answer. Veir fingers felt into another secret pocket inside veir tunic, where vo kept a little store of dried seedpods that came from a certain tree that grew by a bend in the river downstream from the fortress. Tree eggs, vo called them in veir own mind. Vo selected one and began rolling it between thumb and fingers, pressing it, feeling it give. If vo pressed only a little harder it would split open, revealing the pale kernel within. This private ritual was another method vo used to cope with the burden of the presence of other humans in veir life.

"Nemtori, you have to choose a new name! You know how these stinking sheep-eaters treat those who take the middle path. Do you want to spend the rest of your life cleaning up other peoples' filth? You would make such a pretty girl, and how about Lari for a name? I think you should—" but then Quartz stopped speaking, because there came a clatter and a clank. The door shuddered on its hinges, then creaked open. Red light flared in patches through the millet-sacks, bright in the gloom. By the sounds, two or three people were entering. Whoever they were, they brought a torch.

Almond could see in Quartz's face that he thought it was servants sent for stores, and that he was forming an idea to rise with a shout from behind the sacks, or some other such foolery. The two had a private sign language, adapted from one used by the Irzemi guards. Almond made, with trembling fingers, the sign for silence. The skin around Quartz's eyes wrinkled—he objected—but before he could make a sound, they both froze, because a voice both of them knew spoke.

The speaker was the one person they both feared most in all that stony place: Nak Fikoreh, the dour First Minister. Now that the Lady Omdyun's illness had worsened, everyone knew it was Nak who actually ruled, issuing edicts in her name. Knowledgeable palace-watchers all agreed that when

Her Ladyship died, scheming Nak would attempt to seize power.

"Close the door behind you," said Nak. "No one must hear or know that we meet."

Chapter 3

THE TWO SPIES sat motionless, scarcely breathing. Almond, fearing the betrayal of eyes glinting in the light, silently instructed Quartz, showing him he needed to close his lids by doing it once veirself, deliberately, then opening them again and dipping veir chin. Quartz stared back defiance, but then one of the newcomers thumped down so close on the other side of the sacks that grain dust puffed back, and, instinctively, they both closed their eyes. Quartz made a voiceless huffing sound. Almond chanced the movement of a hand to find connection through touch. Veir finger grazed Quartz's thigh, bare below the breechclout. Vo felt the vibration of the restless muscles and willed veir companion to stay still, begging silence.

There followed some shuffling and grunting, until those on the other side of the sacks had found, it seemed, places to settle. Nak Fikoreh spoke again. "The old crow may linger for some time yet. We must remain vigilant. Nothing must break until she is dead, but then we must act swiftly. Are you sure of your men?"

"Aye, Ruler," said a creaky hissing voice, and Almond recognized it as that of one of Nak's thugs, a slovenly man with an odd cap of smooth hair that shone in the sun. His name was Kretsipom. To his face the Nezel servants were careful to call him "Captain," but behind his back they called him in their own language *i Pukál*, the Beetle.

"And you?"

No answer was audible, but Almond, risking slitted eyes, glimpsed through a peephole the slight shift of a nod. The one who did not speak had positioned himself so that the side of his face was visible, and Almond shut veir eyes again in terror.

The Beetle inspired contempt, but this man, Oreg Ardjelfinz, the First Minister's chief lieutenant and enforcer, inspired fear wherever he went. He was a towering rock-hard mountain of a man with a hairless head and impassive face who, some said, never spoke. Certainly, Almond had never heard him. Those few brave enough to call him anything other than "Noble Ruler" might whisper *i Gau*, the Stone.

Nak went on. "You must be ready, whatever hour of the day or night."

Only one voice answered aloud. "Aye, Ruler."

"You and yours to attend to the feather-hats."

No reply. Almond felt Quartz's leg shift under veir fingers and slitted veir eyes open to look at him. Quartz had twisted his face into a hard scowl that captured something of Nak's habitual expression, and he worked his mouth as Nak spoke again, silently mocking him. "And you to accomplish the taking of the sprig."

Now Quartz's face shifted to an expression combining touches of blankness and servility. He mouthed as the Beetle spoke, "Aye, Ruler."

Then back to Nak-face and a flapping of the jaw for, "You know the signal. Seven fast and hard of the temple bell. Whatever hour."

When the Beetle answered, this time Quartz got the timing exactly right—"Aye, Ruler"—and Almond felt laughter pressing up inside, threatening to burst out. Vo poked Quartz's leg hard to get him to stop. Quartz smirked, but subsided. Almond took in and let out a long breath as silently as vo could, pushing the laughter down.

"Just so," Nak went on. "Go now. You and your men will be rewarded."

"All thanks, Ruler," said the Beetle. Feet shifted and scraped.

"Oreg, a moment more," said Nak. One set of footsteps moved across the cave. The door opened and closed again. The Beetle had been sent away.

Nak sniffed. "What a stupid lout, that Kretsipom. But useful nonetheless."

No reply came from the Stone.

"I've given you the harder task. The old crow's guards are made of neither straw nor water. Once your task is done, I want you also to make sure of the sprig, that odious little worm. See that he is brought here, to this room, and make sure he remains alive under trustworthy guard."

Almond could no longer resist looking again, and watched the silent head move once more. The eyes in that menacing face shifted not at all, for which vo felt deeply grateful.

The two men rose. Shafts of light danced with the passage of the torch. The door opened and closed, and dimness and silence prevailed once more.

Chapter 4

"THE BUZZARD, THE BEETLE, THE STONE," Quartz chanted as, after a cautious exit from the sluice, he and Almond made their way back home. They had whiled away the day in the dim cool storeroom, talking quietly and napping long. "Give me a well-forged blade, and I will best any one of them."

Almond gave him a skeptical look, thinking of the mammoth Stone.

"Even him," Quartz insisted. "Gilku says every man has his weakness. Him and his head like an egg. I would best him."

A quirk of Almond's mouth as vo turned away went unnoticed, which was probably just as well, and Quartz carried on with his swagger until they turn into the Street of Jewels, as those who lived there called it—their wry name for the stretch of hummocky land where the huts of the Nezel castle-servants straggled along the base of its outer wall. The hour of the evening meal had come, and the smoke from the cooking fires rising out of the roof holes mingled with the smells of unwashed bodies, the beasts and fowl they tended, and their rubbish heaps and outhouses behind.

As they picked their way down the lane Almond debated in veir mind whether to suggest to Quartz making a secret of what they had witnessed in the storeroom. Vo understood that the talk they had overheard was dangerous to speak of, but Quartz being Quartz, Almond knew that a hint that he ought to hold his tongue was sure to spur him to wag it. Vo decided not to suggest. Some mention would no doubt have to be made, but perhaps the talk would end sooner if Quartz was not provoked.

As they approached the Nez family hut, Almond heard the nasal honking of the *gazu*, the serpent-snaky horn that Gilku, veir father, and Almond both played in the castle orchestra. Vo rubbed veir face wearily. Gilku wanted one of his children to follow in his musical path, and had insisted on veir learning, but vo had no love for the instrument or the music. That was not the crux of the trouble, though. The traditions of the Irzemi masters dictated that, among adult musicians at least, only men were allowed to play in the orchestra, and lately with Naming and its choices so close Gilku had become more insistent. It took an effort of will to lift the latch and open the door. The same battle always awaited now, when vo arrived home.

At the stone hearth knelt Loshi, mother of Almond and spouse of Gilku, stirring a steaming pot. She banged the ladle on the rim. "Just in time," she said.

"We heard a secret meeting," burst out Quartz. "If they had known we were there . . . " He drew a finger across his throat, gagged out his tongue, and flopped his head sideways.

Gilku set aside his instrument. "What meeting? Where was this?"

"In Almond's secret cave, down the sluice."

"Who?"

"That old grave-robber Nak and a couple of his guards. The Beetle and the Stone."

Gilku tugged at his wispy beard. "Ha! Plotting, no doubt," he growled.

Quartz, robbed of the nub of his news, stood momentarily without words. Almond gave veir mother a look, and Loshi, reading it right, interjected. "Cerach, would you please set the board?" For lack of room the low table for the evening meal leaned against the wall during the day. Quartz, standing taller at the unexpected use of his man-name, moved to obey.

"And Nemtori, dear one, could you please fetch the bowls?" Almond hastened to do veir mother's bidding, and

Loshi dished out one of her many savory stews, this one strong in hot pepper judging by the bite and catch of the smoke. Eager hands tore flat bread. Hungry mouths set to work.

Almond had just come to the conclusion that veir father, at least, should hear what vo and Quartz had overheard in the storeroom, and was pondering how soon such a telling could happen, when a sharp rap came at the door. The family exchanged startled looks. No company was expected, and in the Nezel community neighbors did not as a rule visit during the dinner hour. Gilku rose and went to the door. Almond and Quartz followed, curious and a little afraid.

When Gilku opened the door, they all saw a mysterious figure standing there. A mountain traveler he seemed to be, one of those who lived in the high meadows all through the summer tending sheep, for he was swathed from head to toe in the woolen robes that that tribe wore. Even his face was covered, as though he had been trekking through a sandstorm, with only a glint of shadowed eyes showing through a narrow gap. For a moment the figure stood motionless. Then he raised his arms dramatically and spoke in a grating, unnatural voice, tinged with the accent of his people. "Beware, dwellers of the low hills," the figure cried. "Doom comes to you from the mountains!"

Gilku stepped back in alarm. Almond's quick eyes, however, had noticed something—a scar in the shape of a sliver of moon on the back of the figure's left hand. Vo turned and whispered in Quartz's ear. Quartz laughed, and, to Gilku's surprise, launched himself at the robed stranger and knocked him to the ground. Gilku shouted in alarm, but switched to laughing too a moment later. Quartz's tackle had knocked the face-cloths loose, and they all saw a face they knew, a beloved face.

"Lesru!" Loshi cried, bustling forward to embrace the newcomer as he rose to his feet again. "We did not expect you back so soon."

The family circle was now complete. This was Lesru, Loshi and Gilku's firstborn, Almond's natural brother, a compact and muscular young man. Like his parents he had made the choice of sameness at Naming, and wore his manhood with loose ease. He served as hand on one of the barges that plied the navigable stretch of the Green River, down to its mouth. There was much ferrying to be done, chiefly of wool and wares made from wool, and, on the return journeys, of such goods and edibles as could not be extracted from the dry lands round about. The Desert Fortress served as a crucial link between the sheepfolds of the mountains, farther inland, and the roads of commerce in the direction of the sea.

Lesru helped himself to a ladleful from the pot and found a place at the board, talking as he ate. Tales of shipboard friendship and rivalry were what he brought, and wool trade palaver which, as they say, runs as long as the unspooling of an endless skein.

Then he moved on to news from the docks down at the rivermouth, and Gilku leaned forward intently to ask if there was fresh information from distant Nezel, where the rebels continued their long struggle against the regime that many years ago had overthrown and driven out the followers of Riria Dizdi, the Way. There was indeed fresh news, and soon the two older men were deep in talk of revolution—another endless talk—with Quartz sitting silently by, absorbing every word. Almond, who had heard it all many times before, helped Loshi clean up after the meal. The spinning of schemes to reclaim a stolen homeland continued as the hot night deepened outside.

.

Chapter 5

WHEN THE DINNER dishes had been cleaned and stowed and the board returned to its place against the wall, Quartz was sent to haul water from the aqueduct. Almond grabbed a second set of water-baskets on their poles and moved to follow, but a bark from Gilku stopped ven again. The castle orchestra, beloved of the Lady Omdyun, practiced twice a week in a gloomy chamber in the bowels of the citadel. Gilku and Almond between them were the entire gazu section of the band.

Almond knew better than to argue, but could not hold back a sigh. Veir desire to make music, never strong, had faded away of late to nothing. Nevertheless, Gilku would have his way. Even the sigh earned Almond a glinting scowl. Moving as slowly as vo could get away with, vo fetched veir gazu in its sack, then trailed after veir father around the curve of the wall to the servants' entrance.

The windowless chamber roasted in the stinks of candle fumes and unbathed musicians. Some of the fortress's scattered pack of scrawny dogs lay among the stool-legs. Almond followed Gilku to the back row, slumped in veir usual seat, and sulked.

Gilku extracted his instrument from its sack. Almond sighed again and did the same. The old orchestra leader thumped his staff on the floor and called out the name of a dance tune to warm up on, and the band began to play. Almond concentrated on playing without fault. Gilku kept track of every wrong note, and the more wrong notes, the longer the lecture would be after. By the time rehearsal was over, Almond's lips had gone numb. The numbness would go away, Gilku admonished, if vo practiced more. Behind this rebuke lay a weight of parental hope and expectation: that Almond would practice more, that vo would find a way to love the playing, that in the upcoming Naming vo would choose the path of manhood. Hearing the weight behind the words, Almond kept veir face down. Veir fingers felt into the hidden pocket for a last remaining tree egg and rolled it so that it crackled, on the edge of breaking.

A welcome distraction was provided by Eo, one of the Irzemi musicians. He was a slender lithe youth, a player on the *beinem*, the five-string fiddle. When not playing in the orchestra he worked in the castle gardens and elsewhere—one of the fortress's many general laborers, for there were many workers of both the Nezel and Irzemi races. He approached diffidently and attempted to engage Gilku in conversation. Almond the watcher, who knew so much about so many, knew why. Eo pined for Lesru. Poor Eo; as far as Almond could tell, veir older brother had no idea that his admirer even existed. To Almond, observing all the threads tangled and dangling between the hearts around ven, love seemed a dubious undertaking, less than worth the trouble.

In response to a tentative, stuttered question about whether the rumor of Lesru's return up-river was true, Gilku only snarled. Almond, taking pity, supplied the longed-for information. Yes, Lesru had returned. And did he look well? Yes, he looked well. Up to his usual tricks, playing the part of a mountain pilgrim. A smile of gentle sweetness flickered across the young man's face. Gilku made a pointed remark about someone among the beinem players playing flat, and timid Eo fled.

The exchange had darkened Gilku's mood. "Next time, young one, you hold your tongue," he growled. "Sharing family business far and wide to all who ask."

"Yes, Father."

"Never forget he's a *mekil*."

"No, Father."

"For all he knows our tongue as well as any among the sheep-eaters."

Almond couldn't help a hidden smile at this. Even when Gilku was ill-tempered—which was most of the time—he was fair. "Yes, Father."

Gilku's voice dropped to a grumble, and Almond set to cleaning veir instrument, trying veir best to appear dutiful. But Gilku was not done. "And another thing," he said. "This creeping around in tunnels and such. It isn't safe."

This conversation, too, had happened before. Despite repeated chiding, however, Almond sensed that veir father appreciated veir surveillance skills. "We did hear something important," vo said.

A quick turn of the head betrayed Gilku's interest. "The Buzzard and his plots?"

"Yes, Father."

"What did he say, precisely?"

In a whisper, on account of the many ears around them, Almond relayed the gist of what vo and Quartz had heard, interpreting knowledgeably as vo went. The "feather-hats," as Nak had called them, were the Lady Omdyun's personal guards, a small corps of fighting men fiercely loyal to the Z'Borforeh family. The "sprig" could only be young Lord Zilumek, heir to the Lady Omdyun's throne, the son of her son who had died with his wife in the pestilence when their baby was small.

Gilku pulled his beard. "Aye, aye, no surprises," he muttered. "Still, it is good to know. Seven fast and hard of the temple bell, you said?"

"Yes, Father."

"Very well." Paternal pride gleamed out for a rare once, and Almond glowed. "But."

"Yes, Father?"

"Best not take Felshad on such expeditions anymore."

"I understand, Father." Just as well, Almond thought, remembering the impatient trembling of veir friend's flesh under veir fingertips, and his risky mockery, with swift death an arm's length away. As vo rose to follow veir parent out of the chamber, veir fingers released the last tree egg, softened by veir kneading. As soon as possible, vo must return to the riverbend and gather more.

Chapter 6

THE MORNING AFTER rehearsal, on the way to report for duty, Almond heard from a tearful young servant with the fresh mark of a blow on her face that Lork was once again the overseer of daily tasks. Almond turned aside. Better to risk punishment later for failing to report for duty, vo felt, than to endure meddlesome cruelty today. Also, there was the matter of the nearly empty tree egg pocket. Vo slipped out of a minor side gate and away into the desert.

A brisk walk down-river lay a bend between mounting hillsides where, even in the unrelenting heat of high summer, green rushes and a few tender trees grew along the wet sandbar borders of the water. Long-legged white wading birds could be seen there, as well as a compact little stone of a bird, striped blue and white, that hurtled from bank to bank, pealing out a raucous call. Here could also be heard, if there was any wind at all, a sound rare and precious in that arid place—the rustle of leaves, whispering in air that carried the cool caress of the river's moisture.

Each time vo entered this blessed green place, Almond enacted a ceremony. First vo went to the water's edge, to stand with eyes closed, breathing and listening. Next vo knelt in the river-rounded pebbles and dark wet sand to scoop up handfuls of water to drink; for though it might seem that vo never sweated or became otherwise bothered in the heat, vo felt thirst the same as any other being. Once the body's need was met, vo stood again and scanned from one end of the visible stretch of water to the other, searching out the flittings of life. There, a tall brown bird, stalking through the reeds. There, a ring on the water. There, a cloud of midges dancing in the sunlight. Each new sighting brought fresh joy. Only once these sacred gestures were complete did vo return to the speckled shade of the tree-egg tree to lie with veir back propped against its trunk, and begin sifting through the rock-strewn dirt for the talismans vo sought.

In spring the seedpods were a light green, and when pressed they crumpled softly rather than crackling. By this time of summer, browned and dried, they nestled between pebbles, and there were markedly fewer than when they first littered the ground in a nubby carpet, but Almond knew their ways and had no trouble harvesting a pocketful. This task completed, vo lay back, sighed, and slipped into a doze, watching flash and gloom dance behind veir closed eyelids as the fitful desert wind moved the branches overhead.

After a span, the sound of a voice calling jolted veir eyelids open. Who could it be? Someone on a raft perhaps, making its slow way upstream, poling against the current; or maybe someone approached on the path that meandered along the river. It mattered not which. This place was only useful to Almond as long as no other human was present. Vo scrambled to veir feet and headed back.

As vo came to the last stretch of path before the fortress, just where the first whisper of the daily racket of the place— dogs, fowl, voices calling, the clatter of work—began to mix with the natural sounds of the desert, Almond saw another figure approaching. This was Sarvi, the old orchard-keeper, a revered elder of the Nezel community. In Nezel, Sarvi means "Elm Tree." It was a word without meaning to the Irzemi in their desert, and a curiously graceful name for such a gnarled old root of a person.

The two walkers continued toward each other until they met. They gazed at each other in silence for several heart-beats. Sarvi spoke first. "What news, little nut?"

It occurred to Almond that perhaps Sarvi, an astute observer of fortress life, should hear a telling of what had passed in the deep storeroom. Vo did not feel immediately certain, though, and to gain a little time to consider the question, vo chose a lighter response. "News from the river."

"What news?"

"That there is still some green in the world, Auntie."

Sarvi's mouth twitched. "Pert one." The elder was not without humor, though Almond could not recall seeing ven smile.

"Yes, Uncle." *Auntie* and *Uncle* were alike impertinent. Sarvi was one of those among the Nezel who, at Naming, had claimed the middle way, declining both womanhood and manhood, choosing to keep veir child-name and to continue to use the child-words, *vo, ven, veir,* for the rest of veir life. It was, as Quartz had pointed out in the storeroom, a fraught choice, given that they lived the lives of servants in a foreign land. The Irzemi overlords had rigid views about what they saw as the two—and only two—ways to live in the world, as determined by the body one was born with, and they relegated Nezel servants who chose the middle path to the basest tasks: scouring, slops, burning and inurning the dead. Sarvi had done all of these things.

How did such a one become orchard-keeper? Stay in one place long enough, and no one could remember when you were not there. Bear yourself as though you were noble-born, meet every eye with imperious eye, and who had the will to enforce the law? None in this fortress.

Sarvi leaned close and murmured, "Nemtori, little nut, take good care." Vo leaned closer. Veir voice dropped to a whisper. "Something is amiss. Too many moving in the heat. The taste of thunder in the air." No thunder could be hoped for in the depths of summer. It was months away, if it came at all.

Almond's answer was likewise hushed. "Yes, Sarvi."

"Do not let yourself be seen, if you can help it, especially in your secret comings and goings." Sarvi knew of, and encouraged, Almond's interest in clandestine observation.

The exchange had decided Almond. Vo looked up into those unchanging eyes and said, "There is other news, also," and delivered veir report of plotting overheard in the deep places of the castle.

Sarvi, listening, nodded grimly. When Almond was done, vo said, "It is well you have told me. Who else knows?"

"Only my father, and Felshad."

"It is best so," Sarvi said. "Do not tell anyone else, and we must hope that that boy keeps his tongue in his head." Vo gripped Almond's hair and gave veir head a gentle shake. "Stay safe, little nut."

"Auntie, the frost will blight the lemon trees. Fetch the smudge pots!"

The leathern face twitched. "Pert one."

"Yes, Uncle."

The orchard-keeper glanced around, and, seeing no one, walked on. Almond continued back to the fortress, intent still on finding a place secret enough to let time pass uncontested for at least a little while. Vo recalled another favored spot—an old well-house at the bottom of the rock the fortress was built upon—and headed toward it on silent feet.

Chapter 7

THE WELL-HOUSE was a small stone-walled square room with two high slit windows. It could only be reached by descending a long flight of enclosed steps behind locked doors—the Battlemented Stair. The well, a rough natural hole in the ground, twisted down into darkness. From it, a person with a water-basket on the end of a rope of sufficient length could draw up water, if vo didn't spill it all scraping it up from below. No one came here since the completion of the aqueduct that carried water to the fortress from the reach of the river above the falls.

There was another reason none came here: the *gupurt*, a malign creature said to lurk in the damp depths. Almond had never felt entirely certain whether to believe Sarvi when vo warned ven about the gupurt. Something in the way the old orchard-keeper told the tale, some ghost of a wink, robbed veir warnings of at least some of their force.

And yet if a person leaned over the mouth of the well and listened, vo could from time to time hear sounds that seemed out of place—a soft scrape as of a foot on stone, or what might have been a breath or sigh off in the dark. And once, Almond felt almost certain, a voice mumbling, but too low to catch what words it spoke, or even in what language. Almond mistrusted veir memory of the moment. It had happened when vo was younger, back when veir heart still leapt into veir throat at the mention of the supposed monster in the dark.

Almond came to a seldom-used door. Vo fished into a certain crevice and extracted a key, fitted it into the corroded lock, and opened the door. Vo put the key back in its hiding-place, slipped inside, and pulled the door shut behind ven, then paused. Unexpected sound echoed up the long stairs—the sound of a voice. Almond frowned. Could solitude not be had anywhere, this irksome day? Veir fingers felt for one of the freshly-gathered tree eggs to press and roll. Down the switchback flights vo passed, going to see who invaded veir secret place.

The noise grew louder as Almond descended. Someone was talking, and the rhythm of the talk told Almond that the person was alone. Also, vo could hear, the person was weeping. Almond came to the last turn, crouched, and peered around the corner.

A young Irzemi woman was there. She knelt at the far end of the little room, close by a coil of old rope. She wore a headwrap and a flowing robe in a color that spoke of rare dyes from far lands. This was no common person. This was one of noble blood, it seemed, though there were no women this young in the ruling Z'Borforeh family. Whoever she was, she was in full plaint, gesturing vehemently, then slumping into a shoulder-shaking heap.

The echoes of the place made it hard to hear what she was saying, so Almond gambled on crossing an open space to get closer. Still the words rebounded, impossible to understand. A second gamble, and suddenly the figure stiffened and turned. Almond, caught in the open, froze, then blinked in surprise. Despite the color daubed on the lips and around the eyes, vo saw that the tear-stained face beneath the turban was that of Zilumek Z'Borforeh, grandson of Omdyun and heir to the Gilded Seat.

Zilumek's eyes seemed to come back from a distant place. He struggled to his feet. "What do you do here, servant?" he demanded. His voice came out a shaky mixture of command and continued misery.

Almond understood in a flash that vo must instantly choose, with perhaps veir life in the balance, either to show the usual submission, or to wager on boldness. In veir mind's eye vo saw Sarvi's proud upright bearing and haughty expression, and, attempting to match them, replied, "I go where I please. What do *you* do here?"

Zilumek burst into tears. For a little while he only wept. Then he mixed in fragments of speech. " . . . dying, and she wants me to . . . but I'm not who she thinks . . . none of them know . . . you Nezel people, you don't know how fortunate you are . . . "

The young noble slumped once more to the floor. Almond moved closer. Cautiously vo lowered veirself by the wretched form, reached out a tentative hand, touched a shoulder. The tearstained face looked up. Almond said, "Do you feel the . . . I don't know the word in your language. We say . . . the ache to be a girl. Do you feel the girl-ache?"

Fresh sobs were the answer, fresh sobs and a violent nodding. All at once thin arms wrapped around Almond's body. The hot damp head pulled close. Zilumek clutched Almond, and Almond did what vo could to offer comfort, patting with a gentle hand and whispering soft wordless sounds, through a lamentation that seemed as if it would never end.

Chapter 8

THE WOOLWORKS were the center of industry in the Desert Fortress. Fleece sheared in the mountains was transported down by the mountain travelers in huge sacks and stored until it could be washed, combed, carded, spun, dyed, and woven on great looms into cloth to be fashioned into garments and housewares for the people of the castle, or to be sold down-river. Many Nezel servants and Irzemi workers labored daily in the works.

Native workers held higher place than did the Nezel outsiders. They were the ones who spun, dyed, and wove. It was left to Almond and others of veir country-people to prepare the wool for these later steps. On any given day, old Lifimdi, the wool master, would assign Almond to one of two tasks: washing or carding.

There were parts of both tasks that Almond liked, and parts vo disliked. Washing meant solitude, each washer working at an individual trough, so there was no need to figure out how to respond to the presence of other people, and Almond could relax veir constant vigilance and find solace in busy hands. The work itself, though, was unpleasant, involving as it did the harsh hot lye-water and the back-straining labor of stirring and lifting the sodden mats of fiber with a heavy pole.

Carding was easier on the body, and it involved the chance to learn a real skill and perform it well, which gave Almond pleasure. Vo took pride in the neat fluffy tubes of combed fiber vo produced, called *rolags*. Vo had worked out over time how to make them come out even and airy-light, and vo blushed with pleasure whenever one of the native spinners came to select a rolag especially from veir stock, sometimes with the tip of a chin or a smile, acknowledging veir ability.

What made carding difficult was the nearness of other carders, for they all sat in a row on a long stone bench with mounds of combed wool in front of them. Some were Nezel, ranging in age from children up to adults, and some few were Irzemi girls who, after a short apprenticeship, would graduate to spinning and weaving. One particular Irzemi girl named Telim was Almond's greatest challenge. For some obscure reason of his own, Lifimdi felt it important that carders sit where they were told, always in the same seats, and he was quick with a punishing strap if anyone tried to change position. That meant there was no getting away from Telim; and Telim talked incessantly.

True, there were a few advantages to her endless stream of words. Telim seldom required any response beyond evidence that she was being listened to, so Almond was usually spared the labor of figuring out what to say, though vo had to be careful not to lose the thread. If vo wandered away into veir own thoughts and forgot to nod and murmur agreement in the right places, Telim would notice, and when vexed she had both the power and the will to invent some complaint against the lesser servant that would bring Lifimdi with his strap. Also, Almond's command of the Irzemi language was as complete as it was thanks not least to the ample practice of listening to veir carding-bench companion. And, finally, in her endless monologues, Telim did sometimes drop nuggets of gossip for Almond to add to veir horde of knowledge about the doings of the fortress. Even with these advantages, however, Telim's ceaseless chatter was an ordeal.

It was hardest when, as regularly happened, Telim said things about Almond or about the Nezel people that were wrong or insulting or both, and then Almond faced an awful quandary: suffer the indignity in silence, or force veirself to try to say something.

So it was on Almond's first day in the woolworks after veir curious encounter in the well-house. Telim had gotten onto the subject of what she knew, or thought she knew, of the Nezel religion. "I think it so very strange," she said, accompanied by the rhythmic music of carding paddles scraping, "that you only have three gods. Only three! That's a very small number of gods. We have so many they can never be counted by a mortal, can you imagine that? That's what I would call enough gods, too many to count. But you only have three. And one is a man and one is a woman, and one isn't either a man or a woman. That is so strange." This much was in fact more or less accurate, if teeth-gratingly disrespectful in tone, but Telim was not finished. "And you have that fire-bird person too, who made up those strange rules about how children are born not as boys nor as girls neither."

This was getting more difficult by the moment. Almond, who revered Meb Netál, the visionary founder of the Way, as a prophet and spiritual beacon, felt deeply affronted. "The Bird of the Sun," vo trembled on the edge of saying, in spite of the likely consequences of interrupting or correcting; but vo did not speak, because no opening presented itself. Telim plunged on. "That's the part I don't understand even a little," she said. "How can you make a rule about how babies are born? You make a rule, and the babies come out all smooth down there, and don't grow the parts that make you a boy or a girl until they grow up and decide? How is that even possible?"

This was more than Almond could bear. "It's not like that," vo whispered.

Telim did not hear ven. "And then you get to the, what do you call, the name time or what, and you get your name, and, ta-la-la, magic, the bodies change? I can't believe it."

"It's not like that," Almond said, a tiny bit louder than the first time.

This time Telim heard. "It's not like that? So you're born with boy bodies or girl bodies the same as everyone else?"

Almond already regretted speaking, but there was no stopping the conversation now. "Yes."

"So you're not all smooth down there? I always thought you were all smooth. So which do you have, boy parts or girl parts?"

Almond lowered veir face and did not answer.

"And whichever you have, doesn't that just make you a boy or a girl?"

Almond's ears were ringing. Vo felt as though vo might faint. Vo made a supreme effort and said, "We believe, we have been taught, it is our Way, that we take child names that are neither for girl or boy and keep our . . . our parts down there to ourselves, and when we decide, when we choose our names, we live according to the names we choose, like one of the three of our Gods, woman or man or in between." This was undoubtedly the largest number of words vo had said at one time to any member of the Irzemi race in veir life.

Telim had stopped carding and was gaping at Almond in bald curiosity. "But what about your parts, though? Do they change?"

Under the onslaught of that prying gaze, Almond turned veir face away again and remained mute. To answer would mean to delve deeply into beliefs, rituals, and practices that would require hours to explain. For a long uncomfortable moment the two sat motionless. A phlegmy "ahem" ended the silence between them, making them both startle and look up. Lifimdi was there. He did not speak, but he snapped the doubled strap in his gnarled hands, so that it cracked like a whip. Both young workers returned diligently to their tasks, Telim no less than Almond. Irzemi workers were servants too, and retribution for shirking was severe. Almond sighed out silent gratitude for the reprieve, but it was many minutes before vo stopped shaking.

Siblings in Creation, this is the First Teaching.

I am the Bird of the Sun. I am the Being of Light. Light is, and I am, and in the great Dance of turnings within turnings, all turns to all. All contains and dances around and through and within all. Therefore I am Light.

You are Light.

You also are the Being of Light. Light is, and you are, and in the great Dance all turns to all, therefore you are Light.

We are Light.

Follow with me, Siblings in Creation, further into the teaching. For I am the Being of you, as you also are the Being of me. We are the Being of each other. The spirals of our Beings cannot help but intertwine. Our Dances each alone must dance us all together, for all turns to all. We are each ourselves alone, but we are also each other and ourselves all together, all of us, all ways, all times.

We are all together.

And yet for there to be Light there must also be Darkness.

And in consequence of the same Dance of all within and without all, I am also the Being of Darkness. As you also are the Being of Darkness. As we are all also the Being of Darkness, separately and together.

We are the Being of Darkness.

I am the Bird of the Sun. I embody all. You embody all. We embody all.

We embody all.

I am the Bird of the Sun. I embody void. You embody void. We embody void.

We embody void.

Follow with me, Siblings in Creation, to the end of the Teaching. For though we embody both Light and Darkness, all and void, these are not our deepest, fullest truths, for they are perfect, pure ideals, while we are human, imperfect and mortal. Most of all, therefore, it is the Dance which makes us what we are. It is within the Dance that we become one. Most of all, Siblings in Creation, we embody the Dance.

We embody the Dance.

This is the end of the First Teaching. Siblings in Creation, rejoice.

Chapter 9

ALMOND SLEPT WELL in the heat. Vo found it a matter of accepting the air as it was, the breath as it flowed, almost cooler exhaled than inhaled. Vo lay on veir pallet, skin to air, encapsulated in the heat like a seed in its husk.

Sleeping deeply, vo also woke early, opening sudden eyes into the merely warm air of pre-dawn. The pallet at Almond's side, where Quartz slept, was empty, but a little farther off behind the night-curtain, Gilku's snores could be heard. He managed somehow to grumble even in his sleep.

Staring up at the twig bundles of the ceiling, Almond heard a musical clink and knew that veir mother Loshi was awake. Among other duties she worked as silversmith to the fortress, and in summer she rose before sunrise to light her little smithy fire out behind the hut and get her work done in the coolest part of the day. Irzemi tradition dictated that their dead rulers were carried to their burnings with a silver circlet around their brows, crafted especially for the purpose, and the order had come in anticipation of the Lady Omdyun's passing.

Almond rose, slipped on veir clothes, and padded softly out the hut's only door, then around and back to where veir mother worked. This joining happened regularly. They both loved their early mornings together—a time for just the two of them, though often as not they hardly spoke.

For a span Almond watched silently as Loshi plied her craft. The circlet had taken shape, delicate and graceful, and now she used stamps and punches to emboss upon it the intricate patterns befitting, in Irzemi tradition, a woman of rank. When at last Loshi spoke, her words were little more than syllables laced through breath. "My precious one. Something perturbs your mind."

Almond answered just as quietly: "Yes, Mother."

Loshi kept a steady rhythm with her stamp and hammer. Place, set, tink! Place, set, tink! She let the silence spin out. Then, "Do you wish to speak of it?"

Almond's mouth twisted. Vo looked away.

A maternal hand reached to touch Almond's bare knee. When vo looked up, veir mother's eyes were there, steady and warm.

Almond made a fist and pounded it lightly on the other knee. "I don't know how to say."

"Is it the fear we all have now, with My Lady so close to death?"

"Something of that, yes. But that is not all."

"What, then?"

Almond struggled to answer. Loshi, waiting, chose another stamp and began a new row. At last Almond said, "The Naming."

"Ah."

Almond's fist pounded harder now. "There's a thing I have seen. I cannot tell you all of what it is." Loshi nodded. "But I can tell you that I have seen someone sure about crossing. Someone as sure as Quartz, or even more." Loshi set her tools aside and folded her hands.

Almond struggled a little more. Then the words burst out: "And seeing someone so sure about their path, I feel fresh how sure I am not! And Father wants one thing, and Quartz wants another, and no one asks what I want."

Loshi took up her tools again and bent over them once more. Place, set, tink! The question formed between them, until, in the brightening air—behind the hills, the sun had risen, though the light would not strike down on the castle walls for an hour yet—it was as though it had been asked.

Almond whispered, "I don't know yet for certain what I want. I can't make any answer feel right inside me. But I wonder . . . if I might stay in the middle, like Sarvi. I wonder how it would be if I kept the name you gave me."

Loshi smiled.

Almond took up a scrap of solder-wire and began bending it into different shapes. "But, if I do, Father will be so angry. He wants a son to play in the orchestra with him. And Quartz too. Quartz wants me to be a girl. And it would be the end of wool work for me. It would be the beginning of a life of harder treatment, so much harder, from—" vo waved a hand toward the castle.

"It is a hard, hard choice," Loshi murmured, her eyes soft with love. "You cannot please everyone, no matter how you choose." When she went on, it was in a whisper so faint Almond half-fancied vo only imagined it: "But who can you ever please if you do not first please yourself?"

Chapter 10

MANY CRAFTSPEOPLE AND LABORERS rose in the early morning to get their work done before the fiery sun crested the hills. Down at the river dock, the loading of the barges began as soon as there was light enough to see the bales as the stevedores pitched them across.

Both the pitching and the catching took two hands, so Quartz—assigned by an overseer careless of such details—could not help, but anyone who dared to hint that his presence was anything less than crucial had better be ready for a fight. This morning he sat perched on a bollard, calling out frequent advice as to the technique of throwing, the correct distribution of weight in the hold, and the like. The dock workers grinned and offered mock salutes.

Closest to Quartz among the line of catchers on the barges stood Lesru—close enough so that between bales they could talk in undertones not heard by the others.

"How could someone not know?" Quartz demanded. He usually sounded vehement, but there was an extra edge this morning.

Lesru opened a quick mouth to make a joke, but then stopped. His face went somber. "Lad, you are sure," he said. "Ever since you have been old enough to talk we have all known that at Naming you would choose to cross, to claim manhood. But that does not mean that another also has to be sure."

Quartz wagged his head impatiently. "I can see her. Lari. Inside, just ready to be."

"Are you speaking as a friend, as one like a brother, or something more?" Quartz blushed. Lesru laughed. "Ahhh.

That puts all in a different light. You have a hunger for this girl.”

Quartz growled, but didn’t deny it.

“A girl who doesn’t even exist. At least not yet.” Lesru caught a bale, stowed it, returned. “You need to be careful,” he said. “There are more ways forward from this moment than one. Not all of them involve anyone named Lari.”

Quartz visibly wrestled with whether to say the next, but then it came out: “Will you talk to ven? Help me convince ven?”

“You know that is against the Way. Each must choose and declare veir path alone.”

“But can’t you see her? I can, so clearly!”

Lesru took time to answer. “Lad,” he said at length, “I look at my dear sibling Almond, and I see a bright spirit, a tender heart, and a fierce will. I see a wild creature, hard to catch and hold. Like a bird.”

“Like a girl!”

“No, listen. Nemtori is . . . different. In some ways, vo seems too young, too much still like a child to be coming into veir Naming. In other ways, though, vo already seems too old. I have a feeling of ven as someone on the outside looking in.” Lesru’s face had gone a little sad. “Watching us, loving us, but from a small way apart.”

“That doesn’t matter! I want—” Quartz began, but got no further. Lesru darted out a quick hand, grabbed Quartz’s shoulder, and yanked. Quartz toppled from the bollard into the water. Raucous laughter along the pitch-line accompanied his splashing back onto land.

“What did you do that for?” Quartz demanded when, dripping, he had regained his seat.

“Cerach, you have much still to learn of love. It is not only what you want. It is not a taking.”

Quartz scowled. “If you are such an expert, answer my question: how can someone not know?”

Lesru darted out a hand again. It was a feint, not a real pull this time, but Quartz, dodging, almost fell a second time. Lesru shot him a look under bristly brows that said, "Cease." Quartz subsided.

Another cycle of tosses went by. Quartz picked at crystal facets in the stone of his post. When Lesru was idle again, Quartz said, "What of the rebellion?"

"What of it?"

"You said last night there have been defeats."

"Yes, that is what I heard down-river."

"Our fighters are dying."

"Yes."

"And here we idle away our time in this land of sheep's droppings," Quartz said bitterly.

Lesru cast a quick glance down the line, making sure none of the Irzemi workers had heard this slur against their land. "Hush, now," he whispered. "Remember some of them know our tongue."

"I feel so useless!" Quartz burst out. "The Naming is put off, and put off, and all I have in front of me is a life of slavery, guarding hen-houses all through the night and sweeping their stupid temple, and I hate it! I want to go and fight!"

One of the other workers had dropped a bale in the water. Under cover of the splashing to retrieve it and the whistle and crack of the overseer's whip, Lesru stepped close, seized Quartz's shoulder, and put his mouth next to his ear. "Listen carefully," he hissed. "And do not speak when I am done. Sometimes to be a man, it is to keep counsel. Say you will be silent, or I will not go on."

Quartz nodded.

"I form a plan," Lesru whispered. "When the Lady Omdyun dies, there will be trouble and confusion. The guards will be busy with the struggle after, on one side or another. In that time of turmoil I intend to break away. I will travel down the river, day and night, never sleeping, outpacing any pursuit, and come to the ocean-wharves and seek passage north to go join the rebels and fight against the regime to re-gain our land and to bring back the sacred rituals of the Way. We will reclaim our heritage and live free once more." The two young men stared into each other's eyes. Quartz was not breathing. "Do you want to come with me?"

Quartz swallowed and nodded. The fracas around the dropped bale was ending. It was time to get back to work.

"Swear you will speak of this to no one."

"I swear."

"You will want to. I know you. So full of whatever you are full of in the moment. It comes out. You work your tongue too much."

Quartz's cheeks got color, but his gaze did not waver. "I will be a man," he said. "I will speak of it to no one. I swear."

A whip-tip snapped in the air nearby. They were holding up the line. Lesru gripped Quartz's shoulder hard enough to hurt, then returned to work. Quartz remained silent until the barge was fully loaded, his gaze uncharacteristically inward.

Chapter 11

STILL NO WORD CAME from the tower. The window in which attendants would hang the black cloth when the Lady Omdyun had breathed her last stared out from the high wall like a blank eye. The dusty little castle retracted under the inferno-blast of the sun like an old tortoise. Only the endless scratch and buzz of the desert insects broke the silence. It was too hot to sleep, too hot to eat, too hot to do anything but lie in the shade and sip hot river water from the water baskets and wait for death.

One figure moved through the heat: a sickly-looking soldier-boy with helmet askew, stumbling down the Street of Jewels using his pike almost as a crutch. No one sat outside to help him find the right hut, and he wavered uncertainly, casting from door to door. Swaying in the middle of the lane, he croaked into the burning air, "Ho there, vermin. I am sent to fetch one among you." Nothing stirred. The soldier moaned and nearly toppled. "A young one. The one who plays the serpent-horn in the orchestra."

A door cracked open, no face visible in the black it revealed. A voice hissed in heavily accented Irzemi: "The house at the end." The soldier shambled on.

Loshi clutched Almond's hand as they watched through the cracks between the thin sun-bleached boards of the hut wall. "What do they want of you?" she whispered.

"I don't know."

"Say only what you must. Not a word more."

"Yes, Mother." Almond would not have been able to say why, but vo felt calm. It was the heat, perhaps. The hotter it got, the lighter vo felt, until in the broiling noontime vo sometimes felt as if vo could turn invisible and float away, having become no more than a hot breath veirself.

Almond gently extracted veirself from Loshi's grip, fished out a tree egg to hold, opened the door before the soldier could knock, and looked steadily into the sweat-beaded, blotchy face.

"Are you the one I am sent to seek?" the soldier demanded.

"Yes, Captain."

Up close, the soldier smelled as well as looked sick, putting out a sour tang that made Almond's throat work. Vo made no sign, however, and followed the required three paces behind, veir bare feet making no sound. Around the curve of the wall they passed, through the main gate, and on through the ornate archway Almond had never entered, the one that led to the quarters of the ruling family. Veir pulse quickened, along with veir senses and mind. Vo thrummed with wary curiosity.

No bare stone corridors here—mosaic and tapestry adorned the passageways. Woven wool rugs softened the floor. Despite the glare from the windows, at regular intervals small oil lamps burned in recesses in the wall. Now and again a servant could be seen hurrying past, or scrubbing with precious water what seemed to Almond already spotless tiles. The soldier led ven up a curving flight of stairs and stopped at an imposing door fashioned from great beams. No trees this large grew anywhere near. The wood must have been lugged down from the mountains or brought up-river from even farther away. Only nobility had wooden doors as massive as these.

The soldier leaned gasping on his pike for a moment before lifting the heavy iron knocker-ring and letting it fall. The clunk echoed back down the stairs. A bolt could be heard being thrown back, then a latch being lifted. The door swung open. A native-born Irzemi servant wearing the robe of an attendant to the ruling family appeared. Nezel folk were not considered worthy to wait in person on royalty. "Is this the one?" he asked. His voice and face alike were hostile.

"Yes."

"Very well. You are dismissed."

The soldier turned and shuffled away. Almond and the attendant were left gazing at each other.

"What is your name, worm?"

"Nemtori, Captain."

A voice spoke from inside—a young voice, but one clearly used to command. "Bring. Bring here." The attendant opened the door wider, and gestured for Almond to enter.

The door led into a richly appointed apartment. Bright colors dazzled Almond's eyes. In cages hanging here and there vivid flecks of birds hopped and twittered. Heavy wooden furniture crowded the space. An ornate filigreed lamp fashioned from beaten copper hung from a chain in the middle of the room. It was lit, and from the floral reek in the air, Almond guessed that the oil was scented. Cloths hung in the windows, and Almond knew that servants were kept busy through the heat of the day, wetting them down to try to bring some cool to the room. Also, some of the water from the aqueduct was diverted and passed through this chamber, flowing along a channel set into the stones of the floor. The room felt, if not cool, at least a little less sweltering than everywhere else in the palace.

It was Zilumek, the young heir, who had summoned Almond. No trace of his girlish finery remained, no touch of paint. He wore the pantaloons and vest of his station, and his haughty gaze did not so much as flicker as it passed over Almond's face.

To the attendant, Zilumek said, "Go now."

"Lordship—"

"Do not argue. Take the others and go."

"As you command, Lordship." The attendant gave Almond a malevolent look, gathered a few more servants from the next room, and exited. Almond was left alone with the person who, the last time they met, had sobbed in veir arms—and who, with a word, could have ven killed.

Chapter 12

A LONG SILENCE PASSED as the two looked at each other. Almond forced veirself to hold the other's gaze. It was the same decision as in the well-house, taken just as instantly—to meet and treat as an equal. Nonetheless, vo sensed it would be presumptuous to speak first. The noble one had summoned. Let the noble one begin the talk.

After a span Zilumek looked away, but not in a manner that showed weakness—with a small grimace, rather, as though pained. "What's the use," he muttered. He slumped into a large high-backed wooden chair. "My life is over before it can begin."

"You are about to become ruler," Almond ventured, speaking of course in Irzemi.

"Yes, I am about to become ruler." Another long silence, which the young royal broke by barking harshly, "I could have you tortured, you know! I could have you executed!"

Almond stepped back but forced veirself to hold the other's gaze, to answer calmly. "Yes, Noble Ruler. I know."

"Don't call me that!" Petulant, he sounded now, his mood shifting moment by moment—gusty wind painting patterns on the surface of a river.

"What do you want to be called?"

Zilumek brooded. When he looked up, his face looked miserable. "In your Way..." He faltered and fell silent. Almond waited. "In your Way, you Nezel people, you have a name just for when you are children."

"Yes."

"What is yours?"

"Nemtori. It means 'Almond.'"

"A nut. What a strange name."

"The names for children are like that. Simple words for things in our lives. My friend is Felshad. It means 'Quartz.'"

The other returned to brooding. At length he looked up and pointed toward one of the many cages in the room. Inside it, a morsel of bright color flitted. "What is your word for that bird there?" he demanded.

Almond stepped forward to make sure vo was seeing clearly. "*Dimki*. Finch."

"Call me that."

"Yes . . . yes, Dimki."

For the first time, Finch's face softened. Not quite a smile, but a lessening of the stern haughtiness. "Finch. I like it. Finch."

"And then," Almond said, guessing the direction Finch wanted the conversation to go, "when we have our Rite of Naming, we choose the name we will carry all the rest of our lives."

"And you can choose a woman's name or a man's name."

"Yes, Dimki. Or, some choose to keep their child-name forever."

"And when you choose a woman's name or a man's name, it doesn't matter which kind of name other people think you should choose, based on...based on..."

"Based on the body you were born with?"

"Yes."

"You understand aright, Dimki. You can make the choice of sameness, like my brother Lesru, or the choice to cross, like my friend Quartz."

Suddenly, Finch sobbed—one harsh bray of sound, followed by a visible effort to regain self-control. "You're so lucky!"

Almond couldn't suppress a glance around the richly adorned room. Finch read the look and said sharply, "I don't care about any of this. I just wish I had the choice to cross."

For a few breaths they stared at each other. Almond found the way to continue. "Do you know?" vo asked softly.

"Do I know what?"

"What name you would choose."

The thin chest heaved—clearly the question had inspired more emotion. Almond took another step forward and cocked veir head. "Jiom," Finch whispered.

Fortunately, Almond knew enough about the Irzemi to know that this was a girl's name, though it sounded nothing like it in Nezel. "That's a pretty name," vo said, experimentally.

The dam burst. Finch remained slumped in the chair, but gave vent to a squall of tears. Almond glanced anxiously about, fearing the return of attendants. The distressed noble's position made awkward a repeat of the gentle touching that had happened in the well-house. Almond contented veirself with moving the last step forward and reaching out a hand to pat a hand. Finch looked up at the touch. "I just want to be a girl!" vo wailed.

Almond took the hand, squeezed it. "Jiom," vo murmured, and the other nodded, still sobbing.

Eventually Finch subsided to sniffles. No attendants had come. Vo sat up straight, wiped veir eyes, and stood. Haughtiness returned to veir face. "Nemtori, you will come with me," vo commanded.

Chapter 13

FINCH LED ALMOND out a low side door into a deserted passage. After peering both ways to make sure no one was watching, vo pulled back a tapestry to reveal a small door. Almond's quick eyes recorded from which of the many ornamental recesses Finch's hand took the key. The door opened into a dusty narrow hallway. Almond felt for the candle stub vo kept in veir pocket, but it was not needed. As in other passages around the castle of which Almond was already aware, the corridor was dimly lit by narrow slots cunningly worked here and there between the stones. The floor was strewn with grit. In the close, echoless air, Finch whispered, "These passages connect the family quarters. No one is permitted here except those of royal blood." Almond responded with a catch of the breath. "And those who accompany us at our command," Finch added, and Almond had to be content with that.

A turn to the right, a turn to the left, and they came to another door. Finch pulled out a key on a chain around veir neck, worked the lock, and turned the latch. Almond took in another sharp breath. "Do not fear," Finch said. "No one ever comes here." They passed through into another bed-chamber. The windows were covered with heavy dry hangings thick with dust. Dust blanketed the few scattered pieces of furniture, and the floor too. It was plain to see that only a few feet had trod these flags in many years. The path they had made ran from where Almond and Finch stood to another door opposite. The chamber was stifling hot; but that was the same as everywhere.

Finch spoke in a dreamy tone. "These rooms used to belong to my mother and father. No one has lived here since the pestilence took them." Vo led the way across to the other door, opened it, and went through, beckoning Almond to follow. The portal led to a new room with one narrow slit window for light. Many ornate garments hung along both walls, in between tall dust-covered wardrobes. They had entered the dressing room of a woman of the noble house of Z'Borforeh. Finch walked the length of it to the brighter patch of stone below the window, opening wardrobe doors in passing to reveal ranks of sumptuous dresses, and turned again at the end to face Almond.

Nemtori had long ago learned to keep veir face still in the presence of nobility. Invisible service was the rule here, harshly enforced by those who oversaw the labors of the place. Nonetheless, vo could not keep from a widening of the eyes. The person standing before ven was utterly transformed. A shy radiant young woman stood there, her eyes shining. "Isn't it wonderful?" she said, and for the first time in Almond's presence the young noble smiled.

Almond smiled back. "Is there a glass?" vo asked. Reflective surfaces were another rare luxury in the Desert Fortress.

"Oh, yes," said Jiom, and she pulled aside a cloth to reveal an oval mirror.

Having grown up in the Way, enjoying the freedom it provided to experiment with different modes of being, Almond knew more than a little about the pleasure of the trying on of selves. With unfeigned enthusiasm, vo asked, "Which is your favorite?"

The young woman wriggled with happiness and pulled a gown from a wardrobe peg. "This one. It's so beautiful. Wait until you see."

Gone was any difference in rank. They were two young humans in a secret place, joined in absorbing play that brought them both joy. They paid no heed to the passage of time, and for a span nothing else mattered but color and shape, drape and cut, ornament and texture of rich attire lovingly crafted and preserved. Almond had never seen so much opulence of dress, and exclaimed and praised wholeheartedly.

After a timeless time, the light outside the narrow window began to fade toward the colors of evening. It took Almond a couple of tries glancing at the window in a pointed way to jostle Jiom out of her blissful reverie, but once she noticed Almond noticing, she understood. Her face crumpled.

Reluctantly, the young noblewoman removed her last costume and donned again the pantaloons and vest of veir assigned station. With the change in clothes came a return of the stern face, the air of command. Silently they made their way back to Finch's chambers.

The same attendant as before turned as they entered and glowered at them both, reserving a particularly venomous look for Almond. Zilumek made the Irzemi hand-gesture requiring deference. The penalty for a servant who failed to respond properly was death. The attendant and Almond both fell to the floor. "You," said Finch to the attendant. "I gave you no leave to enter again. Go and do not return until you are called, or it will go badly with you."

"Yes, young master," the attendant mumbled into the floor. He rose and hastened out.

"And you, servant," Zilumek continued. Almond flinched at the hard word. The magic of the secret room, it seemed, stayed in the secret room. "If you speak a word of what has passed to anyone, the punishment will be swift and harsh. Now, go from me." Almond rose to obey. Before vo could take more than a step, however, a knock came at the door.

Chapter 14

FINCH GESTURED to Almond to move into the corner least visible from the entrance, strode to the door, and opened it a crack. "What passes here?" vo demanded angrily. Another voice spoke, one Almond did not recognize. There was a brief exchange. Finch said, "You will wait," and closed the door again. To Almond vo murmured, "You must hide." Vo scanned the room. "There. Under there," vo said, pointing at veir enormous bed, remarkable in a land of pallet-sleepers for being raised on sturdy legs with a space underneath.

Almond, all spying instincts roused, obeyed with a will. Vo moved first toward the near edge of the bed, but stopped again at a huff from Finch, who pointed impatiently. The meaning was clear: if you go under there, you might disturb the carpets, or leave traces in the dust. Almond nodded, veir face conveying honest admiration at this finesse of spycraft. Vo hurried around the bed and dropped to the floor in the narrow space between it and the wall. Rather than sliding and scraping on the stones, vo levered veirself on knee- and elbow-points to the precise middle of the bed, then lowered veir body noiselessly to the flags and lay motionless on veir stomach, head turned to watch what little vo would be able to see of the coming encounter.

Zilumek's elegant bare feet paced again to the door. "You may enter," he said, and through the door came the heavy sandaled feet and leg-bindings of one of the soldier class. Almond had one instant to wonder if vo could be guessing right, and then the guess was confirmed. "Oreg," Zilumek said. "What business do you bring that cannot wait?" And now Almond heard what vo had never heard before: the voice of Minster Nak's fearsome lieutenant. The Stone could speak after all. And, almost, Almond failed in veir long training, only barely containing a laugh. The voice of mountainous Oreg was a reedy tenor, light as light on leaves.

"Ruler," said Oreg, his tone hushed but urgent. "I must speak with you on a matter of life and death, and there is only a little time."

Finch's answer was similarly hushed. "Here, come away from the door."

The two sets of feet moved closer to the bed, and closer together. A shift and leaning of weight hinted at a mouth held near a listening ear. Under the bed, Almond concentrated on soundless breathing. "Ruler," Oreg said, hardly above a whisper, "I do not know if you know, but I served your father when he was a boy. When we were both boys. We were about the same age." A wordless sound from Finch: never mind what I know, go on. "When he was dying he called me to him and asked me to watch over you, to make sure you stayed safe." Finch's feet repositioned, as though vo swayed for a moment with emotion. "So have I done, without putting myself forward where it were best I did not go. But now I must put myself forward, because your life is in danger. I have been charged by Minister Fikoreh with assisting in the taking of this fortress when your grandmother dies."

Finch drew a sharp breath, but the heir's voice was steady as vo said, "This news does not surprise me. I have long suspected Nak of dark plottings."

"Ruler, I will help you. But I think it best that we wait until the crisis. Minister Fikoreh's signal is a striking of seven fast strokes on the temple bell. That is when Kretsipom and his men are supposed to seize you, and I to make sure that the deed is done."

"Seven on the bell."

"Yes, Ruler. And I cannot linger longer. When you hear the bell, let us find each other as quickly as may be, and then we will hazard what we can."

"So be it."

Then for a moment Almond was in grave danger of being discovered as Oreg prostrated himself on the floor before his ruler, showing reverence. The side of his face was clearly visible to the watcher under the bed. If he turned his eyes . . . but he did not. Finch's voice said, "Faithful Oreg. Thank you."

"It is my duty and word long ago given, Ruler," said Oreg. "But I would serve you, even if I had not promised your father."

"Faithful Oreg. When we have defeated Nak, you shall be Captain of my Guards."

"All thanks, Noble Ruler. And now I must go."

The guard pushed himself back to standing. Almond fancied vo felt the floor tremble at the planting of those mighty feet. The sandals exited. Ten royal toes flashed and curled as Finch returned to the bed. "You may come out."

Almond crab-walked out, rose to veir feet, and faced the other. Their eyes met. For a moment, in unspoken discussion of what had just passed, they were equals once more, bright young minds calculating new information, new consequences. Then Finch's face went distant again, veir voice cold and imperious. "My prior command stands doubly strong now, servant." Almond dropped veir gaze, suddenly afraid of this young human's lightning-quick changes of mood. "If you speak of what you have heard here to anyone, it will be your life to pay."

Almond knelt in quick reverence, rose again, and fled. There would be no sharing of intelligence gathered with veir father this time. Thinking of Gilku's suspicious mistrust of all the Irzemi people, not to mention his volatile temper, Almond knew it would be best not to mention anything at all about the day's happenings to him, no matter how heavy the weight of the secrets vo now had to bear.

Siblings in Creation, this is the Second Teaching.

Hear now the Teaching of the Vision of the Three.

For I heard a deep calling. It was the time of longest day, so that night was banished, but in the dim of the smallest hours when all slept, I woke in my chamber as though a voice had summoned me. And it seemed to me that all sound had vanished from the world, so that in a hush like that of a dream I rose and stepped to my window, that looked north toward the lands that in winter are all one vast forever of ice and snow. Now in midsummer they glimmered and faded into the far reaches of mystical Light, and still there was no sound. Every fold and contour of all that land lay before me, dressed only in the short dry grasses that grow all the summer long. And that was passing strange, for in waking time such meadows lie further north, on the far side of birch forests.

Then, still without sound, I was lifted up and carried softly down from my window through the luminous air and set down at the head of a track leading north into the deeper wilderness. I knew that the call I heard in the stillness of my soul required me to walk this path, and so I set forth.

How long I walked I cannot say. Perhaps it was only a little time, though it also felt like an eternity. At length I knew myself to be in a different land. Behind me the path faded and I knew that the only way to go was forward. At last, I came to a place where three figures stood.

They wore plain garments without ornament, all the same. The wind that blew through the grasses moved their robes. They stood without speaking, at the points of an equal triangle, facing in toward each other.

I looked at their faces and forms, and in the Light that shifted and moved it seemed to me that likewise their faces and forms shifted and moved, so that I could not feel certain that I saw them clearly. The face of the first seemed first the face of a woman, then the face of a man, then the face of one neither woman nor man, but someway in between, both or neither. The face of the second likewise shifted and changed, and likewise the face of the third.

I felt the desire to know who these strange figures were, who did not speak or seem to know that I was there. Presently, though no voice spoke, I did know: they were the Three. And when I knew this it seemed to me that the face of the first became lighter in its features; and the face of the second became more pronounced in its bones and forms; but the face of the third continued to change and shift as before. And then, though still and forever no one spoke aloud, the sacred words formed in my mind. Each of the Three in turn was revealed to me.

Chapter 15

ONCE A MOON OR SO, Sarvi came to dinner at the Nez hut, staying after to sip bitter cactus brew with Gilku and discuss palace doings and, sometimes, to play the game of monarchs. When the board and pieces were brought out, Quartz always noticed. Since Sarvi had taught him how the pieces moved and what one must accomplish to win the game, the boy had yearned to best the old orchard-keeper, who was by far the strongest player in the Nezel community. He had never figured out how to it. Almond knew the rules too, but seldom played, having no taste for the direct contest of wills. Vo was content to watch.

The next such visit had been set, as it happened, for the evening of the day of Almond's summoning to the royal chambers. For the first game after the meal, Sarvi demonstrated the flaw in an early gambit of veir father's. Gilku played an eccentric game, indulging in flights of fancy, but when they were shown to be unsound, he tipped his monarch with a rueful smile and a quip. Almond felt comfortable watching the two older humans play, because they never lost track of the game being a game. Vo felt less comfortable watching Quartz at the board, because veir same-as-sibling played with a fierce intensity that flared into temper when he made mistakes, and especially when he lost. Just at the moment, however, Almond craved the comfort of nearness to veir elders more than vo feared vibrating in sympathy to Quartz's anger, so vo pulled out a tree egg and stayed.

Against Quartz, Sarvi played with veir usual measured care, but also indulged in running commentary, half gentle teasing, half instruction. "When are you going to learn, young one?" vo asked as vo built with care a defensive wall. "Always

"

rushing in headlong. No patience." Quartz never answered except with moves, though one could judge whether the talk was reaching him by how sharply the pieces hit the board. "Look, young one, at the whole field. What of your own camp? You come swashbuckling in, and never think of the balance of the position. Do you remember what happened last time? You threw away one piece, and then another, and, yes, there were chances here and there to gather something back, but you never thought long enough to see them. Easy now! You'll upset the board."

"Ah! Again you attack! Look, again I say, at the whole field. Where is the rest of your army? Some still stand on their starting squares. They cannot arrive in time to take advantage of the breach you have torn in my line. And observe this pawn—you have left it entirely undefended." Sarvi moved one of veir pieces to the square occupied by one of Quartz's, removing it from the board. Quartz punched the side of his head and uttered a muffled curse, then raised his fist over the board. All three of the others in the hut reacted with sound or movement, and Quartz froze. His eyes flitted from face to face. Abruptly, he bolted to his feet and lunged out of the hut. The door slapped shut behind him.

Gilku, Sarvi, and Almond exchanged glances. This had never happened before. They could hear Quartz just outside, his voice too low to catch words. By the tone, he was berating himself. Almond moved to rise, wanting to follow and offer comfort, but at a sign from veir father vo sat again.

At length the door opened, and Quartz came back in. Almond observed the line between his eyes, the tightness of his jaw muscles—but also, less familiar in those often-stormy features, a deliberate stillness. Quartz took his seat again, leaned over the board, and pondered it, motionless. Something in veir friend had changed, Almond saw, and vo waited curiously to see what he would do next.

What he did next was to find a move that made Sarvi startle slightly, then settle over the board and ponder in veir turn. When vo returned to veir banter, veir tone contained a touch of wonder. "Well then, what's this? A bold sally! It is unsound, surely. You lose a second pawn. But, no, see, new avenues have opened. The rest of your army comes hurrying up behind. I must consider the safety of my monarch." Vo fell silent, and when at length vo made veir next move, it was with an unusually cautious air.

Quartz answered deliberately, and the game continued at an unaccustomed slower pace for a span, still in silence. Almond could make no sense of the bewildering permutations on the board.

Finally a position came in which, to avoid the final trap of veir monarch, Sarvi had to give a check to which there was only one answer. Quartz made the forced move, and then Sarvi had another check that drove Quartz's monarch back to the square it had just come from. Sarvi repeated the first check. Back and forth they went, until Quartz looked up questioningly.

"We have repeated the same position three times," Sarvi said, "so it is a draw." Quartz nodded minutely—it was the first time he had not lost to the master. Sarvi extended a hand across the board, and after a moment, Quartz gripped it. "Well played, Cerach," Sarvi said. For once Quartz showed no reaction to the use of his man-name. "It is possible that with best play after your sacrifice, you had me beaten. Fortunately for me, I was able to find the perpetual check."

Quartz nodded again. He asked in a level voice, "Sarvi, have you ever met a player stronger than you?"

Almond was surprised to see something almost like a grin flicker across the elder's face. "Yes, I have."

Gilku paused in his putting away of board and pieces. "You have?" he said. "No one in our community comes close to your skill. Who?"

"When I was much younger than I am now, there was one who would come from time to time to offer a game. And against this one, I could not triumph more than one or two times out of five."

"Where?" said Quartz. "Here?"

"Yes, here in the Desert Fortress."

"Who was it?" Quartz asked.

"A solemn young man, in service to the royal family," Sarvi said. "A subtle player, adept in particular at attack, slow in the building, but sure in the end. And we would talk sometimes, almost as equals, though he was a native of some rank, and I a foreign servant. We would discuss, even as we do here today, the many threads of castle life."

Gilku's eyebrows had bunched. Almond and Quartz exchanged a look. Something about the way Sarvi was spinning the tale hinted at a twist to come. Sarvi rose to veir feet and drained the last of the brew from veir cup. "I would even say I liked him," the orchard-keeper continued. "But then he began to acquire more influence and power with Our Lady—this was shortly after she came to the Gilded Seat—and he appeared less often over time, and eventually no more at all, and I watched him turn hard with ambition and a sense of his own superiority, until no way existed any longer that he and I could meet again as anything like equals."

Gilku shook his head, still frowning. "Have you guessed who I mean?" Sarvi asked Almond and Quartz.

Almond had, but felt no desire to speak. Quartz said incredulously, "You don't mean that buzzard Nak Fikoreh, do you?"

"The same."

"I don't believe you. You said you liked him."

"I did, in that time. Not for many years long since. Now I only fear him, and oppose him." Then farewells were said and Sarvi departed, leaving behind an unusually quiet Nez family hut.

Chapter 16

IN THE RICHLY APPOINTED royal apartments the heir-apparent to the Gilded Seat, ruler-in-waiting to scrub and heat-waver and rocks and furtive desert creatures, stared into a mirror. Under veir breath vo sang a wordless nonsense song, the same scrap of tune over and over. Each time the ending came back around, vo bobbed veir head in time with it. As vo continued to study veir face in the glass, vo put words to the song: *Dimki, Dimki, I am Finch. Finch I am, I am a Finch. Dimki, Dimki . . .*

Dreamily, vo reached for a colorful headcloth, violet and blue, which vo liked to have near and had therefore pressed into service as a throw over a table. Vo modeled it in the mirror, turning a shoulder, arching veir back. Vo stroked veir own cheek, lovingly, as a mother might. Veir lip trembled.

A knock came at the door. In a flurry, Finch rearranged the fabric on the table, checked veirself in the mirror again—all looking as anyone would expect—turned to the door, assumed veir habitual imperious stance in front of underlings, and called out, "Enter."

The door rattled and swung open to reveal the usual guard, bowing quickly and retreating to admit a small round woman with a lined face: Mibun, the chief of the healers tending the Lady Omdyun. She performed the lesser standing salute. "Lordship, My Lady summons you," she said.

Finch stepped back. From the undimmed haughtiness of veir face, one watching would not know how shaken vo was by this news.

The Lady Omdyun had ruled the Desert Fortress for so long that only a handful there could remember a time before. She had come to the throne while still a girl, after her father, whose only living heir she was, had collapsed in the midst of a rage and died. Korn Z'Borforeh had been an unstable bloody tyrant, given over to his appetites, especially after his young bride died in childbirth. His daughter Omdyun had grown up in the shadow and orbit of his fury.

Many another would have wilted in that harsh soil, but she took root and grew, bearing the brutality when it could not be avoided, and building an inner core of defiant strength. She learned some of her father's harshness, too, developing the capacity to act as severely as circumstance demanded. In all, she matured into a capable leader.

When Zilumek had been small, Grandmother would occasionally send for him, and he would be required to amuse himself quietly in a corner while she sat at her table, commanding and dismissing, reading and signing and stamping documents, receiving and negotiating with visitors. She never showed her grandchild a moment's warmth or tenderness, and he regarded her with a mixture of awe, fear, and adoration. In her later years, never gregarious, she had become remote, unseen by anyone but attendants for many days at a time.

Mibun waited patiently. Finch gathered veir wits and said, "Very well. Let us go."

At the top of the narrow spiral stair, outside the sickroom doorway flanked by two guards with plumed helmets, Finch paused to catch breath. The climb and anticipation alike had set veir heart knocking behind veir breastbone. When vo had regained veir composure, vo gestured to Mibun, instructing her to open the curtain.

The archway opened into a bare stone chamber, circular, illuminated only by the mid-morning sunglare from the one square window. Another attendant sat by the head of the low pallet where the Lady Omdyun lay covered to the waist by a light cloth. She had never been a large woman, and her illness had shrunk her down to a gnarled doll. Her hands on the coverlet, with their swollen knuckles and absence of flesh, looked grotesque. Her face and skull appeared hardly less skeletal. The room smelled of dust, with just a hint of something bitter in the air—perhaps the lingering odor of some potion the attendants had tried to entice her to sip. Her chest rose and fell almost imperceptibly.

Finch approached the pallet, knelt beside it, and took one of the claw hands in veir own. It remained limp. Finch glanced at the senior attendant with a question in veir eyes. "She tried to speak, before, Lord," Mibun said softly. "We thought it was your name she wished to say."

Finch inclined veir head, accepting this interpretation. "Leave us," vo ordered.

Mibun seemed about to speak, then clearly thought better of it, and with a tip of her head instructed her helper to retire with her to the other side of the curtain, leaving Finch and Omdyun alone.

Finch turned back to the bony mannequin on the pallet. "Grandmother?" vo called softly. Vo received no answer. Vo called again. Still no response. For a span the young heir sat motionless, head bowed, holding veir grandmother's hand. Then, in a low, halting voice, vo began to speak.

"Grandmother, I believe that you called me. You have always said and done exactly as you saw right, and never without reason.

"I also believe that you can hear me.

"And, I believe I can guess what it is that you might want to say to me.

"Grandmother, I wish I could remember my father, your son, more than I do. I was still so young when the pestilence came. To me he was a huge face and a voice that . . . that cradled me . . . so that I felt when he spoke that nothing could harm me, ever." Vo stared into a corner, then continued. "I remember little more of my mother. Only that she had long dark hair, and was quiet and gentle."

A longer silence followed as the young noble wandered the chambers of memory. At length vo leaned down to bring veir mouth close to the ancient ear. "But, I do not think remembering the dead is why you brought me here today." Vo swallowed. "I think you brought me here today because you know your end is nigh, and you seek to be assured that I am ready to rule in my turn." On the other side of the curtain, a foot shifted on stone. Could the attendants hear? Finch considered for a moment ordering them farther away, then decided it didn't matter. Stern love flowered in that young chest. A sense of family honor and duty welled up. "Grandmother, you may go easy, if you truly feel it is time for you to go. I am ready to rule in your stead. I am young, but no younger than you were when you took up the Ring and Dagger. I am strong. I can serve in my turn. I can, and I will."

Zilumek jolted back and uttered a cry. His grandmother had squeezed his hand, one short sharp nip.

Chapter 17

WORD FROM THE TOWER was that the Lady Omdyun slowly worsened. Soon, in keeping with ancient Irzemi custom, all but the most essential work would cease, and her subjects would be called to sit in vigil, awaiting her passing in reverence and contemplation.

The bustle of preparation for this time verged on chaos. On the second morning after the game of monarchs, Almond, on the way to work, realized that here was another day when vo could not face the harsh energy of so many other humans under stress. It was time to disappear again.

Vo recalled a concealed door that opened into passages behind the walls of the kitchens, similar to the hidden hallways Finch had shown ven on the magical day of the trying on of selves, though not connected to them. In these passages also, small amounts of light shone at intervals through slots and cracks; and some of these openings in the stonework ran straight enough to provide views of what lay outside. When the watching mood was on ven, Almond found diversion in peering out, in hopes of serendipitous discoveries to add to veir store of castle-knowledge.

Vo found the door, entered, and wended deep into the secret dim once more, checking peepholes as vo went. Out of the first few nothing could be seen but a blank wall or an empty courtyard. The third was more interesting. It offered a view from the side of a small balcony, accessible, Almond knew, only by passing doors habitually guarded. Vo had never seen anyone there, and after one glance prepared to continue on, but then took another look. A familiar figure stood on the balcony. It was Oreg.

The huge man had positioned himself at the back of the balcony, in a narrow slice of shadow, holding himself as still as the stones of which the fortress was made. Curiously, he stood with one hand over his heart, and something in his stance gave Almond the impression that he was watching something or someone.

Naturally Almond wondered what or who warranted such covert scrutiny from the fearsome Stone. The balcony overlooked an inner courtyard where a small kitchen garden grew. Almond studied the angle of the gaze, pictured the layout of the fortress in veir mind, and wondered if another door vo knew might reveal the mystery of Oreg's fixation.

On silent feet the young human with the watchful mind slipped down sweltering corridors, out again into populated quarters. Corner, corner, straight stretch, went the route, and on to a place where a square shaft dropped down, navigable by narrow shelf-rungs let into the stone of one wall. At the bottom, the passage continued around another corner and off down a final hallway, seldom used and poorly lit, that led to the door vo sought.

After a pause to let breathing settle, Almond eased the door open. Up to veir left hung the balcony on which Oreg, it was to be assumed, still loomed. Vo did not bother to look, knowing that from this angle the underside of the balcony was all vo would be able to see. Creaking the door open slowly wider, Almond saw a figure crouched down among the scrawny dry-leafed pepper plants. It was a servant gardening, with only veir homespun-clad back visible—except, when he sat up on his knees to wipe his brow, Almond instantly recognized him. The garden-worker was Eo, the gentle beinem player who yearned to be noticed by Almond's brother Lesru.

Almond studied the slight form, puzzled and intrigued. What possible reason could Oreg have to watch perhaps the most harmless, blameless person in all the fortress? Tender, diffident Eo, who would never hurt anyone or anything—he could never be a plotter or a schemer, for even the most dim-witted enemy would see though him at once. Or so Almond had always thought. Perhaps vo had underestimated the young man.

Or what if it was something else? As part of veir chosen role as an observer in the world, Almond had done veir best to develop an awareness of the distinct vibrations of desire and love. That hand on the heart—it was a gesture out of character for the watching soldier. Could it be that gargantuan rocky Oreg fancied Eo? The young gardener was beautiful, after a fashion, Almond supposed. Vo had heard the old saws, both ways—like attracts like, yes, but also, the one about opposites that draw toward each other.

Picturing the two of them together, Almond almost broke veir rule against making any sound while on the spy-trail. So much bone and muscle on the one side, so much sheer bulk, and on the other, a river-reed switch of a lad. Vo won veir struggle to contain the laugh, after which vo frowned and sighed. The tanglings of both bodies and hearts felt absurd and foreign to ven, but to desire and to be desired—sometimes vo could feel how fine it might be to have these things happen in one's body and mind and life.

Almond had seen enough. Vo closed the old garden door so softly that not even a grain of dust fell. Neither watcher nor watched had become aware of veir presence.

Chapter 18

—LITTLE NUT, what do you do here?

—The majordomo sent me, Sarvi, to work with you.

—Orchard work has never been your task before. Speak, young one. Why do you not look at me? Do you tell an untruth?

—Please don't send me away!

—So. Weary of fetching and errands, are you?

—Yes, Sarvi.

—Weary of orders.

—Yes, Sarvi.

—Of all that they want of you. And of this long waiting under which we all suffer. You seek a little time to just be.

—Oh, yes . . .

—Well. Very well. So do I come here too, to be with my trees. In days of trouble, it does a person good to have somewhat to care for. But you must work.

—Yes, Sarvi.

—These trees, if my Lady loved them any less, they would long ago have perished in the heat. The work is hard and hot, little nut. We must carry water from the aqueduct. Thirsty, they are, these trees.

—I will carry water for the trees, Sarvi.

—Very well. Fetch the basket-poles.

—Sarvi?

—Yes, little nut?

—Will you . . .

—What is it? Take care, you spill.

—I'm sorry, Sarvi.

—Better. Easy now. What would you ask?

—Will you tell me of the old country? Of Nezel?

—Hum. You ask me to remember.

—Is that . . . does that hurt you, Sarvi? To remember?

—Yes, it hurts. It has been so long since we were driven out, and I begin to fear that all my years will unfold before there is any chance that I may go back. The Regime is so strong.

—I am sorry, Sarvi.

—I too am sorry. But also it is sweet to remember. Stay silent long enough, and I yet may. Very well. Let me see. Nezel. Well. You know, it is a green place.

—Yes, Sarvi.

—Stay silent, young one. Let my mind travel . . . Green. So green. In spring the birch trees leaf out all at once. One day you see the same bare branches as all the winter through, though the furry buds hang heavy with the new life within, and the next day it has burst forth. And such delicate leaflets at first, a green so light it is almost yellow. A different yellow, though, from that of autumn, half the year around. Little nut, again you spill! There is no need for haste. Better to arrive with full baskets than a little time sooner. What was I saying? The yellow of autumn, yes, it has its own clear beauty. And to stand on an afternoon of sun and cloud in a grove and hear the yellow leaves whisper in their trembling all together, like countless tongues that seek to tell their secrets before the long deathly cold comes down again, it is a joy. But the yellow of the new leaves of spring, it is like no other. It is like the sun if we could look at it without it burning away our sight. Like the morning of the world . . .

—Sarvi?

—Little nut?

—You stopped speaking.

—Did I?

—Will you tell me—

—Soon I will have spoken enough.

—Yes, Sarvi.

—Oh, very well. Will I tell you . . . ?

—Of winter, Sarvi. I have never known cold, and I wonder so much how it would feel.

—Ha! You might not like it, such a desert creature you have always been, waking to liveliness when all others wilt. Do not be bashful. I have seen you. It is a strength to take pride in, that you can move through the heat as you do.

But, yes, winter. Cold. So cold. It bites the hands and feet in spite of all the spinning and weaving and knitting all the year round. And hunting and planting and growing and reaping and storing of food must happen all the year round too, for a winter without enough to eat is cruel—each day colder and darker, bringing the dread of frozen famine.

And yet it was the dark that was worst. At least, I will say so for myself. I never minded the cold so much. It bit my feet, but still, to stand under the high white sky in the clear twilight, the air burning your throat and your breath coming in great clouds as you looked out over a snowscape all in blues and greys—that also was a joy.

But, the dark. The sun would rise hours after a working person must be up, tending beasts or chopping through ice for water or fish, all in starlight. And when the sun finally did rise, it seemed so old and tired it could hardly lift its head before laying it down again and going back to sleep in the cold. Sometimes in the darkest time, even young and strong as I was, I lost sight of hope.

A little like now, here, though the sun burns so bright every day. Hope gets lost different ways at different times. And, ware, you spill again. Enough talk. You came to find a little time in which to breathe, but still the trees thirst. I will end and say, the dark is one thing I do not miss. The light here, it warms a person from within.

And yet still I pine, always, for home.

Chapter 19

BACK IN THE WOOLWORKS again, sitting on the rough stone of the carding bench, making rolags for the spinners, Almond for once felt slightly less uncomfortable sitting next to chatty Telim. The never-ending flow of talk was still an ordeal, but on this occasion there was a specific item of gossip vo was interested in extracting, if Telim was in the know, and the puzzle was how to get her to reveal it. Direct questions felt risky. They would seem unusual, and seeming unusual would attract notice, not only from Telim, but perhaps also from wool master Lifimdi, who on this day was in a particularly rancid mood, snapping his strap and muttering as he walked the line of workers. Every few minutes he would poke his nose close to someone's laboring hands and make peevish remarks about the work. Insults or a blow of hand or strap often followed. The long tension of waiting simmered through the castle just as the ceaseless late summer heat did. Tempers frayed. It was dangerous to get oneself noticed.

Further complicating the situation, Almond knew that the nugget of information vo prospected for, if true, would seem scandalous, even taboo, to the young Irzemi servant. Among the Nezel people, love of a woman for a woman or of a man for a man was accepted as one of the natural consequences of the teachings of the Way. From Meb Netál's first insight that all humans were born simply human, free to choose their path in life as woman or man or in between, it followed with a simplicity of logic a child could understand that likewise love was love. Anyone could feel tender stirrings toward anyone, and in the teachings of the Bird of the Sun, those stirrings were regarded as precious and sacred—a view Almond whole-heartedly endorsed, even if, so far at least in veir young life, vo had never felt such stirrings veir-self, nor seen their absence as a lack. Vo did still get pleasure from speculating about their presence in other humans.

So the puzzle was how to nudge Telim's chatter in the direction of Oreg and Eo. The more Almond had thought about what vo had seen in the garden, the more vo wondered if there could be something there. It was not hard to see how someone might conceive of a fancy for Eo. When he knew he was being observed he seemed ill at ease, but when he did not know that anyone was watching, he had a gentle grace.

At first it seemed a hopeless case. Telim's topic of choice was the old ruler dying in the tower. For the last several years the Lady Omdyun had existed as a presence more felt than seen in the Desert Fortress, and in the absence of any more than scraps of real information about her, the communal myth-factory of gossip, superstition, and wild imagining had not been idle. "Do you know what they say?" said Telim. "They say that she can send out her spirit, which is invisible, so that no one can see, and that her spirit walks the passages at night, looking in on us as we sleep. Her feet make no sound and she can pass through doors and walls too, so you never know if she is there or not, and any time you wake up in the night, when you are lying there on your pallet in the dark, she could be right there, watching you."

Normally Almond would only nod and make a small sound of agreement in response to a story like this, but vo wanted to try to direct the flow, so vo murmured, "That's scary."

Telim looked momentarily startled to hear Almond speak, but accepted the remark. "You might think that, I sup-pose, being one of the heathen bird-people," she said. "If she found you wanting in some way her wrath would be terrible for you. But we are her people, and she loves us. She watches us to keep us safe, to protect us. I will be sad when she dies. But won't it be different when her grandson comes to the throne! He's not much older than I am, or maybe even the same age. Can you imagine being the ruler? With fancy clothes and a room with a stream running down the middle of it and pretty blue and yellow and red birds in cages, and all the apricots you can eat whenever you want to eat them! And guards with feathers on their helmets standing outside your door with their spears. How funny that would be!"

Telim set aside a rolag and reached for another clump of wool. Almond leapt into the gap. "They don't—" Telim gave ven a sharp glance, and Almond changed what vo had been about to say to a question, although vo already knew the answer. "They don't all have feathers, do they?"

"Who, the guards?"

"Yes." This was the longest actual conversation these two young humans had ever had.

"No, they don't all have feathers. Only the ruler's special guards have feathers. All the other guards and soldiers have regular helmets, or go bare-headed. And they have sandals with ties that come up around their legs, and some of them wear the symbol of the Dagger as a sign of the house of Z'Borforeh on their chests. I think some of the soldiers are quite handsome, don't you? So big and manly. They will protect us if enemies ever come, but what enemies could come? We are alone in our desert, and even the mountains—"

"What about..." For a moment the two stared at each other. Almond had never interrupted before. Down at the end of the room, old Lifimdi lifted his head. Afraid vo had gone too far, Almond blurted, "What about that Oreg? Do you think he's handsome?" Then vo dropped veir eyes and made a hasty show of getting back to work.

Telim took another agonizing couple of seconds to answer, but then Almond heard the rhythm of veir companion's carding resume and breathed a little easier. "Oreg!" Telim said. "No, I don't think he's handsome. He's too big. And he never talks or smiles. Some of the guards are funny. My cousin Silot is an underguard, and he tells us stories. He doesn't like it when Oreg is in command, but it doesn't matter any more, because Oreg is gone." Almond glanced up at this, and Telim noticed and said, "Oh, yes, haven't you heard? Minister Nak called for Oreg, yesterday it was, and sent him away on an errand. Silot told me. Down to the city, I think, to carry a message from our Lady to the palace of the Preceptor, or some such. Silot didn't really know. But the guardroom is buzzing with the news, because it seems strange, they all said, to have such an important captain gone with our Lady so close to her eternal reward."

Almond was hardly listening, and all thoughts of extracting further information about possible romantic yearnings from veir talkative companion had evaporated. Seeking gossip, vo had stumbled across real intelligence. Oreg sent away! Nak must have suspected him somehow, vo thought. Poor Finch. The young ruler's chances of surviving the coming upheaval, slim to begin with, had just become slimmer.

Chapter 20

AT LAST, THE ORDER for vigil went out—no work, except the few most essential tasks, until Lady Omdyun died—and Almond, in veir endless quest for space and quiet enough in which to breathe freely, fled once again to the green bend of the river, seeking bird-love and water-love. It was early morning, and vo had some hope of a good stretch of time in solitude.

Vo enacted veir ritual of arrival and settled under spindly leaf-twittering branches, but before vo could get properly started on the task of sorting through pebbly rubble for tree eggs, a slight out-of-place sound caught veir ear. Something or someone not usual moved among the jumble of boulders just downstream. Almond's gaze darted to the spot, in time to see a human head lift up above a curve of stone. Vo startled, but subsided again. It was Eo, and in another second Almond understood that he had been fishing, for as he made his way among the stones it could be seen that he carried rod and net and a string with three silvery fish-bodies hanging from it. Almond would still have preferred to be alone, but if someone else had to be there, let it be gentle harmless Eo. Vo held still, waiting for the other to see ven.

The young man approached, his face creased with care. He did not notice Almond until he was only a few gravel-crunching steps away, and when he did notice he gasped and jerked back. They stared at each other for a moment, and then Eo said in Irzemi, "Nemtori. I greet you."

"Eo. Likewise I greet you."

Eo scanned around them, as though checking for listening ears, stepped closer, and squatted down, laying his burdens on the ground beside him. "It has been a morning of strange encounters," he said. "That is why I jumped."

Almond answered with a tilt of the head.

"This morning when it was still dark, I came to be in this place. The fish rise before the dawn, and I am more hungry than the ration they give can satisfy." Eo glanced to see if Almond understood the import of this remark: Eo was defying the ban on work. Almond moved veir mouth a little to convey that the young Irzemi servant's secret was safe with ven. Eo nodded. "I came over the wastelands, avoiding the path for fear of meeting someone it would not be good to meet. I was crossing a dry watercourse and, coming around a bend, I spied another person in the ravine with me, or so it seemed. It was still almost full night. If I did not dream it, this person was tall and thin and stooped, moving away. An elder of our Irzemi people, I might have said, if I had seen the same figure in the fortress. But out in the desert in the dim light, I could not be sure."

They shared a pondering silence. Eo went on: "It is not permitted to speak of such things in the Temple of the Innumerable, but in the stories we Irzemi tell we speak of the dead returned, not in body, but in spirit."

Almond said, "In our stories, we tell of such also."

"And some believe that when they appear it is to bring news of great change, whether for good or ill."

Almond nodded. Eo lowered himself from his squat to a seated position, legs crossed. Almond sat up from the bank and likewise folded veir legs, so that they faced each other as easy equals. Almond said, "Do you believe the stories?"

"It does not take a spirit to tell us that great change is about to happen," said Eo.

"No, that is true." Almond looked away, discomfited at the reminder of the many troubles unavoidably to come. When vo had taken a breath to calm veir mind, vo glanced again at the other's face and saw it working. Some deep feeling, it seemed, moved under the surface, perhaps seeking expression in words. Almond wondered if vo was about to be asked about veir brother Lesru. But when Eo spoke again, vo was surprised by what he said.

"You Nezel folk, in the eyes of many of my people, you are the lowest of the low."

Almond forced veirself not to drop veir eyes, and searched the other's face. Vo saw there a mix bashfulness, sympathy, and naked pain. "What you say is true," vo said quietly.

"I am sorry that it is so," Eo said. "And I know that they are wrong." The young man looked down at his hands, which had become involved in tugging and twisting a length of fishing twine. He kept his eyes down as he went on. "But they do not pass their judgements only on your people. Among ourselves also the Irzemi have many hard thoughts about each other, and many hard words to give those thoughts shape and force." Almond nodded again. Vo knew how many of the Irzemi of all ranks found repugnant the more fluid ways of the Nezel with regard to sense of self; and Almond could understand how others of Eo's race might look upon his slender lithe grace and mild ways and conclude that he partook of some of that fluidity.

"Yes, I have heard some of the words they use," Almond said.

Eo went on, "And it may soon become worse. There are many in the fortress . . . " He stopped and gave Almond a probing look. "Yes," he said, "I believe I can trust you. There are many in the fortress who fear that when our Lady passes through the veil, Nak Fikoreh will seize power. And if he does it will go badly, I think, for all you Nezel people, as well as for those, like me, who do not fit their ideas of how a person should be and . . . and love. For Nak has a particular hatred of anyone who is not a man born boy who loves a woman, or a woman born girl who loves a man. He has expressed it often, and he has contrived persecutions and punishments for those who transgress."

Almond, watching the emotions flicker across the other's face, felt a warmth toward him, and wondered: should vo tell the young man about what vo had witnessed in the garden? About Oreg's burning stare from the balcony? Would this news bring Eo joy, or pain? Or both? Vo pondered a moment, then shook veir head. Vo did not feel certain of the meaning of what vo had seen. It was best not to speak of it.

Another thought followed on the heels of the first, though: Here was one who truly seemed an ally. The Lady Omdyun could live but a day or two more, and Eo did not know what Almond had learned about Nak's plots. Vo was in a position to confirm the forebodings the other had just expressed. Should vo bring the young man into the circle of those who knew? Vo must decide now, for in the distance footsteps could be heard. Someone else approached along the river path.

Almond studied the lovely fine-boned face for another instant, seeing there no guile, only a steady thoughtfulness and solicitude for others. Vo decided, and spoke in a hurried whisper: "Listen, Eo: there are indeed plots. Old Nak does wait for our Lady's last breath to try to seize power. Hidden in the deep storeroom, I heard him giving orders to Oreg and Kretsipom. But I also know—I do not have time to tell you how—that Oreg means to help Lord Zilumek when the crisis comes, and it seems that Nak must suspect as much, because he sent him away. The signal to spring the plot when our Lady dies is seven on the temple bell, and Lord Zilumek is to be taken alive to the deep storeroom, and ... I cannot say more ... " The footsteps had almost arrived, and Almond realized from the particular driving pace of them that it could only be one person who approached. Vo had one moment to sit away from Eo, who stood and stepped away also, before Quartz crested the rise and descended the bank toward them.

Chapter 21

OF COURSE QUARTZ KNEW the riverbend too. The two friends had come here together often since childhood. Some other time he and his boisterous energy would have been welcome, but not today. Almond couldn't help scowling, but took care to compose veir expression again before veir hardly-less-than-brother was close enough to see.

Eo gathered his fishing things and made a hurried exit, brushing past Quartz with a wordless sound that might have been greeting or apology or both. Quartz gave him a dismissive glance. As Eo moved away over the rise, the young Irzemi man cast an intent look back at Almond. Perhaps he sought to convey response to the whispered intelligence of a moment ago? But Almond could not read the look. Vo could only hope vo had not erred in sharing the news, especially the part about Oreg's intention to help Lord Zilumek, which, despite having been ordered not to tell anyone on pain of death, vo had impulsively added. Meanwhile, this other human must be reckoned with.

"What was he doing here?" Quartz asked, a tinge of contempt in his voice.

"You saw. He was hungry. On short rations during the vigil."

"And defying the ban," Quartz said, his face showing pleasure at the thought of power over the other.

"You leave him alone!" Almond said, with unusual vehemence. Quartz gave ven a surprised look, and Almond noted a subtle difference in veir friend's face. What was the change? He seemed older, somehow. Harder, but also more contained. Something of his mien and manner after the game of monarchs had taken longer than momentary hold, it seemed.

Quartz broke the stare between them first, with a nonchalant shrug. He bent down to take up a stone and turned toward the river. He knew better than to aim at any living thing while Almond was present. The time he had injured a heron, vo had not spoken to him for eighty-one days. He threw his rock instead into the middle of the river. Kerplunk! He took up another stone. Kerplunk!—again, in the same spot as the first. His aim was sure. Ripples spread.

The first two stones gone, he squatted down and scooped together a small pile, settling into the pastime he had chosen. "You're not the only one who can find things out, you know," he said as he worked. He glanced to see whether Almond was listening. Vo was.

"Because of the vigil I didn't know what to do, so I was walking around inside the castle wall, and I came to the orchard. Old Sarvi was there." Kerplunk! "Vo was sitting on one of the stone benches under the boughs, and vo had a basket there on the bench, and was filling it with food." Kerplunk! "I saw a flat loaf and some quinces and what might have been a jug of olives." Kerplunk! Quartz glanced again. Almond was listening intently. "Vo couldn't see me. I hid behind a corner of the wall, watching through a joint between the stones. When vo had filled the basket, vo went to the place where the wall of the garden meets the wall of the fortress, and did something I couldn't see, and a little door opened there, and vo went in, leaving the door open just a crack." Kerplunk!

Quartz had thrown his last stone. He came and sat down by Almond, kicking up sand. Almond moved a little away, and another brief expression of pique crossed veir face, though vo once again took care that the other not see it.

"So I waited a little while, and followed. The door opened to steps going down, and another door at the bottom opened into another larger, longer flight—"

"The Battlemented Stair?"

"Yes. I followed as quietly as I could, remembering what you've taught me, and I came to the last turn into the well-house, and found a way to peek around the final corner without being seen, and what do you think old Sarvi was doing?" Almond shook veir head. "Well, you might not believe it, but vo had tied that basket of provisions to the end of the big rope that is always there, the one they used for hauling water before, and vo lowered the basket into the well."

This was unexpected and astonishing information. For a moment Almond was a child again, alarmed and delighted in equal measure. "Feeding the gupurt?" vo said.

Their gazes connected, and for a moment they savored together the echo of a shiver from younger days; but then Quartz said, "That's just a tale they tell."

"I am not sure. I have sometimes thought I heard sounds."

"Sounds," Quartz scoffed. That could be anything, his tone said. Sand sliding. Water dripping.

Almond didn't press the point. "What happened next?"

"I got a tickle in my throat and made a little sound. Sarvi didn't look up that time, but I thought vo would if it happened again, so I left. I didn't see anything else."

They sat together in silence for a spell, the feeling between them more companionable now. Almond pondered this fascinating fresh intelligence. What could it mean? Could the gupurt be real? Or was the recipient of the basket some other creature or person? That was more likely, after all, than some supposed evil monster always spoken of with a ghost of wink, but never seen. If a person, then who? Vo wondered whether it would be advisable to ask Sarvi about what Quartz had seen . . . but veir thoughts were interrupted. Quartz had put his hand on veir hand.

For a hot buzzing moment Almond stared down at their two hands on the ground between them. Then vo looked toward veir nearly-sibling's face. It was turned carefully, artfully away. A small drama was being staged. If I am not looking, the angle of his cheek said, no one can tell I am touching you.

Almond scrambled up to stand away. At the motion Quartz turned his face back to ven. His new composure had broken apart into an expression of baffled longing. Neither spoke, but their bodies said all that needed to be said.

Quartz's body expressed the restless pungent joy of being young and alive and vital, full of emotion and desire. Under the surface sheen of caution in his eyes, an eager hunger burned.

Almond's body expressed the pain of savage pulls in opposite directions. Toward the ardent youth, not returning passion, but loving all the same, and wanting more than anything not to hurt. In conflict with that, and winning by swift degrees, the innate desire and need, felt since vo had had mind enough to feel and say what vo was feeling, to be left alone. For several heartbeats vo writhed on the pin of veir dilemma, then spun and fled.

"Nemtori! Wait! Come back! Why can't you . . ." Quartz trailed off into a snarl of frustration. Almond was already gone.

Chapter 22

NEMTORI SPENT the rest of daylight hiding in a desert bolt-hole so secret only vo knew of its existence, but as darkness fell, thirst and hunger edged out the discomfort that would come from the risk of seeing Quartz again, so vo returned home. As vo approached the hut, vo stopped at a distance and strained to listen. Vo could hear voices. It was Loshi who was speaking, and something about her tone said someone else was there who was not a member of the family. Almond crept silently closer, until vo could discern words as well as tone, in time to hear veir mother say, "Revered One." Almond exhaled and dropped veir shoulders. Vo knew who the visitor was, and the knowing made it safe to enter, whether Quartz was there or not. Almond took the last steps to the door, opened it, and entered veir home.

Quartz was not there, which was still a relief even with the safety provided by the family's visitor: Meji Kaz, the Nezel community's Officiant, their spiritual leader and keeper of the teachings of the Way.

Meji was a tall, heavy woman who moved and spoke with a stately grace befitting her station. Her voice, dark-toned and low, reminded Almond of the lowest notes of the gazu. She oversaw the spiritual doings of the little refugee community with a calm authority born equally of her absolute devotion to the Way, and a natural sense of her own importance. Almond loved her, feared her a little, and found deep comfort in her presence.

Almond's parents and their visitor were sitting on the ground around the low table. The remains of a meal were there. Nezel holy ones seldom had to cook for themselves. Almond went first to the water basket, tipped out a small portion to wash veir hands, then drank a thirsty ladleful, and another. Next vo went to veir mother for a quick embrace. Finally vo turned to face veir Officiant. Vo put veir palms together and held veir joined hands out, and Meji placed her hands around them, pressing them gently—the traditional greeting between spiritual follower and leader. "My child," said the Officiant, in her soft rumble, "it is good to see you."

"And you, Revered One."

Meji Kaz looked searchingly into Almond's face, and Almond wondered if the Officiant was about to raise the subject of the upcoming Naming. Vo fervently hoped not, because it would be hard to answer the questions that might be asked with Gilku there, but vo respected veir religious leader too much to object and held veir breath. The Officiant said gently, "Nemtori, you must be hungry."

"Famished, Revered One," and with that it felt within the bounds of proper respect to sit and eat.

Whenever Meji Kaz visited the Nez family hut, Almond found it diverting to watch veir father struggle to contain his usual irascible self. Gilku Nez believed devoutly in the Way, but being mostly made of pepper, he couldn't seem to find another way to express himself. So it was on this occasion. As the conversation began again, it became clear after only a few words that there was disagreement between veir father and the Officiant. It had to do with a question that had been the subject of much debate in recent days among the Nezel servants: what were they going to do when the Lady Omdyun died?

To some it seemed inevitable that Nak Fikoreh would rise to power, and, fearing new as yet undreamed-of persecutions, they argued for flight. Better to run and take their chances wandering in the desert lands, they argued, than to face Nak's cold cruelty. Meji Kaz was one who argued such.

By contrast, Gilku Nez was one of those who held that, even though they were refugees in a foreign land and toiled in servitude, still they had homes, and families intact, and a strength of community that should not be thrown into jeopardy due only to anxious imaginings. Stay, went this line of thought, stay and fight if need be.

"Revered One," growled Gilku, "you don't . . . I think it is possible that you don't . . . that you may not fully understand how harsh this land and its heat can be." His fingers reached up to tug at his beard, but he looked at his hand and put it back down on the table.

"It may be so," Meji answered calmly.

"When I was younger, I was pressed into the gangs that labored on the aqueduct, and it was such work as could kill a man." Meji was nodding sagely. "It did kill a man, two men, before it was done. One of ours, collapsed in the heat and passing the next day in a fever, and one of the sheep-eaters, dead of an apoplexy." Gilku's fingers, no longer in his conscious thought, strayed to his beard again. "So can't you see it would be madness . . . that it would be ill-advised to venture into the desert? We have children among us, and aged ones, and those who are infirm."

Meji held up a hand. "And yet—"

Gilku made an impatient sound in his throat. Loshi laid her hand on his arm. He scowled and dropped his eyes.

"And yet," Meji resumed, unperturbed, "I fear more what is likely to pass should we remain. On all roads forward from this moment there is peril."

Gilku nodded, head still down. Almond nodded too. It was true, what Meji said. Vo felt inside veirself the burden of suspense, a burden which all in the fortress shared. It was exhausting to know that upheaval was coming, but not when it would come, or what form it would take when it did.

"What I can never forget," the Officiant went on, "is the savageries of those of own nation when our beloved Meb Netál was overthrown. The pitiless execution of whole families, even down to the smallest child. Nak Fikoreh is such a one. I have seen him in a Meaningful Dream, and his hands were red with Nezel blood."

Gilku failed to contain a scoff. He was a faithful follower, yes, but that did not prevent him from taking a dim view of some of the more mystical aspects of an Officiant's practice. Almond recalled other occasions when veir father had expressed skepticism in response to the idea of Meaningful Dreams, calling them too convenient to the ends of the dreamer to truly be of divine origin.

The least expression of annoyance flashed across Meji's face, then was carefully smoothed away. She opened her mouth to continue the debate, but was interrupted by the sound of approaching feet. Knuckles rapped sharply on the flimsy slats of the door.

Chapter 23

A SHARP LOOK passed around the Nez family table. With talk of cruelty in the air, each saw in the eyes of the others the same quick fear. Had the persecutions already begun? The knock came again, louder. A deep Irzemi voice cried out, "Ho there! Come out. You are summoned!"

Gilku put two fingers to his lips, counseling silence. The heavy knife for cutting up fowl lay on the sideboard. He took it up and stepped to the door, holding the weapon behind his back. He opened the door. "Who is summoned, Captain?" he asked with forced deference. "And who summons?"

"You and your child are summoned," said the soldier. Almond rose silently and went to a knothole that vo knew gave a clear view of the space in front of the hut. Vo recognized the soldier as one who usually had gate-guarding duty, knowing him to be a rough but not necessarily unkind or dangerous man. "And it is my Lord Zilumek who does the summoning. You are to bring your serpent-horns to our Lady's chamber."

Gilku pulled his head back inside, saw Almond close by, and waggled the knife, still held out of sight of the soldier at the door. The message was clear: take this from me, it is not needed. Almond took the blade. Gilku turned his face out-of-doors again and said, with actual deference this time, "We will prepare as fast as we can."

"Be quick," said the soldier. "I am to return with you both as soon as may be. That is what my Lord commands."

Loshi had already moved to take the two gazus in their sacks from their pegs on the wall. Meji Kaz looked on silently, her face alert. Gilku stepped behind the alcove-curtain to change into his ceremonial tunic. As Almond changed hastily into veir own tunic, vo voiced a hope. "Do you think that this means that our Lady has taken a turn for the better?"

"No, young one," Gilku said. "I think it is young Zilumek who seeks to ease his grandmother's passing." His voice was unusually gentle. His next words surprised his listeners, so loath was he usually to say anything positive about any of the Irzemi race. "It is nobly thought of. A fine gesture."

Almond had only seen the Lady Omdyun a few times. Vo regarded her with awe. She had ruled for so long that it felt as though she had always been there—a force of nature, one of the elements, rather than a mortal human woman. Her turning out to be mortal after all had shaken everyone in that fortress to some degree, Almond not least. In a distant way, vo loved the Lady.

Vo therefore took up veir instrument in its sack if not eagerly, at least purposefully, thinking for once of playing veir best. If a little music would ease the great woman's journey toward whatever came next for the Irzemi after death, rejoining the Uncountable Holies or what ever it might be, then Almond would play the best vo could.

It was not the full orchestra that was summoned to play. They could never fit in the sick chamber. Gilku and Almond were there, and Eo and another beinem player. There was also the elderly man who played the little Irzemi double drum, and one or two others—a chamber ensemble, hauling their instruments up the spiral stair.

When they entered the room, passing between the plumed guards, only the motionless Omdyun and one attendant were there, dim in the glow of a single oil lamp. The attendant sat near the window, and Almond noted with a pang that the black cloth sat folded on the sill, ready to be hung.

In the absence of the ensemble's usual leader, it fell to Gilku to choose the tunes and set the beats. He named a melancholy sweet song to start. No singer had come to sing, but the words spoke of young love lost and yet also the joy of being alive. Next Gilku named a bouncy dance number. In her younger years, the Lady Omdyun had loved to dance, and later she had presided over the dancing, waving her hands as she watched the bobbing figures in the smoky hall.

For a moment Almond felt uncomfortable playing such a jaunty tune in this deathly place, but then something shifted in veir heart, and vo strove to play as musically as vo could. The gazus were featured, as it happened, in this tune, honking out the jagged melody. Almond noted veir father's rare look of appreciation and quailed inside. Now Gilku would have fresh arguments regarding the fitness of gazu-playing as Almond's path forward through life. But it could not be helped. To bring music into the dying woman's dark solitude, that was all that mattered.

As the dance tune ended, Zilumek entered and stood quietly by the door. His demeanor was all distant command. Glancing at him as vo played, Almond could not tell whether he gave ven a look before turning his steady gaze back to his grandmother on her pallet. If he had, it was too quick and veiled to be noticed by any other there.

Gilku had of course also noted the young lord's entrance, and when the dance tune was done he offered obeisance: a bow, and a murmur that might have included syllables of Irzemi honorifics. Zilumek inclined his head in return. To the assembled musicians, he said, "Thank you for playing for my grandmother. There is one tune in particular I know she loves. Play it now." Then he named a ballad so old that the Irzemi had one set of words for it in their language, and the Nezel another in theirs. Gilku bowed once more, accepting the order. He turned to the little band and counted out the tempo, and they began.

In this song the gazus accompanied, and Eo had the melody. He was a talented musician, possessing the ability to bring genuine, heartfelt emotion into his playing. He did so now. Eyes closed, swaying to the aching, calling phrases, he brought singing out of his instrument a gorgeous sorrow. Almond felt strongly moved. The ancient tune as Eo played it seemed to ven to express a tender hurt too deep for words to express. Almond felt that hurt in the core of veir own being, and sensed it vibrating also within the humans around ven.

Suddenly Zilumek strode to the pallet and knelt down. Surprised by the sound of movement, Eo opened his eyes and faltered in his playing, and in the moment that his bow halted on the strings all there heard a quiet creaking sound, as slight as the songs of the tiny wrens that hopped among the thorns in spring. The Lady Omdyun was humming.

"Don't stop!" Zilumek ordered. "Play on!" The musicians struck up again with a will. Eo returned to the melody with, if possible, even more feeling, a tear tracking down his cheek. Other faces besides his were wet, Almond's among them. The Lady could still hear, could still make sounds with her failing throat. She yet lived, and the music had reached her.

In the silence that followed the end of the song, all eyes were on the young lord, whose attention was still focused on the pallet. The silence stretched. At length Gilku made a small diffident sound in his throat.

Zilumek looked up. "Go now, all of you," he ordered brusquely. But as Almond moved to follow the others, he looked straight at ven and added, "No, not you. You are to stay, and come with me." Almond looked at Gilku's face, and was alarmed to see blooming there a look of suspicion and thunder. Poor Nemtori, strung between hard eyes. Vo risked figurative death by disobeying veir father, and literal death by disobeying the temperamental young prince who knelt by his grandmother's side, holding one of her hands in both of his. Vo stayed.

Chapter 24

AFTER A WHISPERED consultation with Omdyun's attendant, the heir apparent ordered Almond to bear a lamp, then led ven down the spiral stair and back toward the quarters of the ruling family, walking at a steady pace, head high. All they met in the halls moved to the side and bowed. Finch disdained to notice them. Vo marched forward cloaked in an intensity of thought and purpose that, slight of frame though vo was, gave ven an air of majesty.

Almond, pulled along in veir wake, watched the faces recognize, the eyes flick and drop—quick obedience driven by and masking fear. Used to thinking of the one who led ven as a fretful child, Almond marveled. The question came into veir mind of what might happen if they were to encounter Nak Fikoreh. The thought was good for a shiver.

They did not meet the First Minister, arriving without incident at the great wooden door to Finch's apartments. Curtly, not allowing anyone else to speak, Finch dismissed guards and servants, clearing not just the room but the corridor in both directions as far as sight reached. Then vo ushered Almond inside, motioning for ven to shut the door behind them. Almond wondered if vo was about to meet gentle Jiom again. Vo hoped so. That time in the forgotten changing room felt miraculous in memory now, and if a return were possible, it might be a way to be apart for a little while from the trouble that seemed now to rise up everywhere.

Once they were alone, Finch paced to one of many large pieces of furniture in the room, a cabinet with numerous drawers. Almond remained by the door, all senses on high alert. It would be best, vo sensed, not to try to play games of power this time. Vo dared not act the equal. The ruler had ordered ven to appear for some unknown purpose. Vo was a servant and could only wait to be commanded.

At the cabinet, Finch seemed to be searching for something, opening several drawers in quick succession, rifling impatiently through their contents. Presently, it seemed, vo found what vo sought, for vo stood back with a little sound of relief, irritation, or some strange mix of these and other emotions too. Vo turned to Almond and said, "Come here."

Almond obeyed, stepping over the streamlet of aqueduct water in the middle of the room. Seeking just the right amount of autonomy in the moment, vo contented veirself with walking a little slower than vo could have while holding veir eyes steady on the other's face as vo approached. That face had changed yet again, seeming younger, more liquid and vulnerable, as though some aspect of secret Jiom mixed uneasily with the young noble who was the only of Finch's forms of self that anyone else in the fortress had ever seen.

At the cabinet, directed by a gesture, Almond looked down into the little drawer. Among a clutter of baubles and trinkets, Finch's fingers had cleared a space around two stoneless silver rings.

Old, they looked, and neglected, for with the passing of the years they had tarnished nearly to black. Still, it could be seen that some person skilled in silvercraft had labored over them. One of the two appeared slightly heavier than the other, and carried on it no mark or device. The other, a touch slenderer, had been worked with delicate finesse in variations of the same intricate designs that Almond had lately watched veir mother stamp on Omdyun's funeral circlet: the traditional marks of an Irzemi woman of royal blood.

The rings looked like they would have a pleasing weight, but something about Finch's stillness cautioned Almond to keep veir hands by veir sides. Finch said softly, "They were my father's and mother's. Everyone among our noble families gets one, given at a certain point as we approach our grown time. And when . . . and when it is time for a new ruler, we say that the Ring and Dagger go to that person, and the Dagger does—there's only the one Dagger—but the ring doesn't, not necessarily, because you can accept the old ruler's ring, or keep your own."

Knowing the answer, having watched veir mother craft it a year ago, Almond said, "Have you a ring of your own?"

"Oh, yes, somewhere," Finch said dismissively. "Stupid thing." Almond felt insulted on veir mother's behalf, but kept veir face still. "It is as bare and plain as my father's, that one there." Vo pointed at the heavy plain band. "I could take that one, my father's ring, if I wanted," Finch went on, "but it doesn't fit." Vo plucked up the larger ring and slipped it on veir finger. It seemed only a little too large, in fact, and Almond drew breath to say so, but then realized that the other meant something else and stayed mum. With a grimace, Finch took veir father's ring off and dropped it back in the drawer. The dry wood clattered. The caged birds around them added chittering counterpoint. Vo took the other ring, the filigreed one, out of the drawer and fondled it, but did not put it on. When vo spoke again, veir voice trembled. "And this one fits, but . . . it is not permitted. I cannot wear it."

Abruptly vo pushed the lovely blackened trinket into Almond's surprised grasp and turned away, striding across the room to pull aside a window-hanging and stare out into the hot dark. "Put it back!" vo commanded. "I never want to see either of them ever again! Put it back and close the drawer!"

Almond stared down at the small circle on veir palm, then glanced back at Finch, who continued to stare out the window. Quick as the thought forming in veir mind, with no time to calculate the risks involved, vo reached out careful fingers, noiselessly extracted the plain band from the drawer, and, glancing one more—still unobserved—tucked it away in veir spy-craft pocket. Next, vo made sure that the decorated ring rattled as it landed in the drawer. Vo scrambled the contents, so that the absence of the plain ring could only be discovered by a careful search. Vo made sure also that the drawer made sounds in the closing, a creak of wood pushed askew, and the clack of closure.

The ruler-in-waiting left the window, crossed the room, and took up the blue and purple headcloth disguised as a table-throw, running it softly through veir hands. "I had thought . . . one more time . . . " Finch said, and for a moment Almond saw another flash of Jiom in the changeable face. Then she was gone again. "But no. My life is over before it can begin. Do you see?" The words were calm, but spoken with a look of tragic loss in the eyes and face.

"Yes, Ruler," Almond said. The use of the title was not calculated. Vo had spoken from the heart.

Finch stepped close to Almond and held out the pretty turban-wrap. "Keep this for me, Almond," vo said softly. "Then I will know that at least one person knows. Then maybe in a way I won't have to disappear completely." For one more moment they looked at each other. Jiom, Finch, Zilumek—Almond saw them all flicker. Then the other's eyes went distant. The next command came with no particular force, but it was a command all the same. "Go from me now. This was a mistake. I need to be alone."

Almond hastily knotted the pretty cloth around veir wrist, performed a reverence, and hurried out, the silver ring vo had pilfered tapping veir thigh with each step.

Chapter 25

AS ALMOND NEARED the Nez family hut, vo circled to approach a back corner on silent feet, the one vo knew had the fewest gaps between the planks. Veir fingers agitated a tree egg. Was Gilku home? That look of thunder—vo did not know if vo could face it. And what about Quartz? They hadn't met again since the supremely awkward moment at the river. If both were there, Almond would not enter, would disappear instead into the desert. Vo extended every tingling sense.

From the sounds of work and the soft singing, only veir mother was inside.

Loshi looked up with a smile as Almond came in. Almond's response was a tentative but urgent question—the next step in a plan so spontaneous it continued to evolve even in the asking. "Mother? May I ask you to do a task for me?"

"Of course."

"You will . . . you will want to know why, but I cannot tell you."

"Yes? You intrigue me, my love, I confess."

"I cannot even say or give any sign, if you were to guess, whether you guess right or not. It would be best that you not guess at all."

"Very well, Nemtori."

"You will want to guess."

"I will ask you no questions."

Almond stared searchingly into veir mother's eyes before reaching into the hidden pocket. Silently vo held up the heavy, smooth, and tarnished silver ring. Loshi gazed at it in wonder, and with, indeed, many questions in her eyes. Almond watched her struggle with the desire to ask them, and shook veir head minutely. Loshi closed her mouth and nodded, also barely enough to see, but deliberate. Suddenly the situation struck them both as comical, and they laughed a little together. Then, somber again, Loshi whispered, "It's beautiful. What do you want me to do with it?"

Almond moved so close veir lips brushed veir mother's ear as vo whispered veir wishes for this particular piece of regal adornment. Listening, Loshi nodded, and held out a hand to take the precious thing, putting it into a secret pocket of her own.

As she completed the motion the door banged open, and Gilku Nez came into the room, his face wrathful. Quartz was there too, entering behind him.

Almond tried to escape, angling to run around them and out the door, but veir father cut ven off and pinched veir ear. When not playing in the fortress orchestra Gilku did many other kinds of work, including curing sheepskin and shaping stone. His hands were hard as horn. Almond cried out in pain.

"What is this?" Gilku demanded, pointing at the head-cloth still knotted around Almond's wrist. He pulled it off and held it up. His face contorted. "What disgrace have you brought upon this family?" he bellowed. "Tell me instantly. Speak, child!"

Almond collapsed to the ground. Gilku had the choice of holding the full weight of veir body by veir ear, or lowering his hand. He lowered his hand but did not relax his grip. "What did our lordling want with you? Answer me!"

"I cannot say!" wailed Almond.

"Speak if you value your skin in one piece!"

"I cannot say," Almond repeated, in a quieter voice. Then, whispering, "It is death to say."

There was a gasping silence. Gilku released his grip and stepped back. Almond remained in a heap on the hard dirt floor. Loshi opened her mouth to speak, but Gilku shushed her. When he went on, his voice was quieter, but shook with emotion. "Did he . . . Was it his wish to claim . . . did he force the choice on you and then . . . " The thought he was thinking so horrified Almond's father that he left it unspoken, but all there knew what he imagined. It was the Irzemi tradition that the noble-born had the right to claim as consort any servant they wished. To be thus selected meant, in the beliefs of the Nezel, permanent defilement. Gilku began to shake. He raised a hard hand. Loshi sprang forward with a cry and restrained him. "So you've chosen your path!" Gilku thundered. "Chosen against my wishes, and let yourself fall into the clutches of that vile sheep-eating mekil!"

Almond's faint "No, Father," went unheard.

"You are no longer a child of mine! Begone! Go back to your harem! Much good may it do you! I disown you! You are not my child!"

The hut was in bedlam. Loshi sobbed as she grappled with her spouse. Quartz shouted angry defiance. Almond scrambled to veir feet and broke for the door, pausing only an instant to snatch veir gazu in its sack from the wall and smash it violently on the hearth stones. Vo whirled and banged out the door.

Loshi and Quartz both followed, but by the time they stood together in the lane, Almond was already a small and distant figure, vanishing into the dark.

Gilku came out behind his family, still stormy of face. "The child is dead to us," he said. But when his spouse turned to face him, his gaze wavered.

Loshi's voice was stony quiet. "You and your temper. Always you assume and act without knowing." Gilku's eyes stuttered away. "To accuse such a thing, with no proof, in such a tone. We don't know what our Nemtori has seen or not seen, done or not done. We don't know." Gilku opened his mouth, but Loshi overrode him. "And now you cast ven from the house, with your bluster and your foolish theatrics. Well,

I hope you are proud of yourself. You'll sleep alone in the hut tonight. I'll be staying with my friend Shadlashu."

Quartz, meanwhile, face even fiercer than usual, had set off running after Almond.

Chapter 26

ALMOND RAN HEADLONG up through the dry scrub and rocks of the hillside at the start of the long wastes that led at last to the mountains. Wordless sounds issued from veir lips, fragments of the wild jangle within. Vo only knew vo needed to get away from all other humans. If any part came through clearly, it was, repeated: "Leave me alone!"

Behind ven came running feet. Almond glanced back and saw Quartz chasing after. When he saw ven looking, he called, "Nemtori! Wait! Come back!"

Almond grimaced, turned ahead again, and ran; but vo could not escape veir larger, stronger friend. His footfalls clattered closer. Almond made one last desperate attempt to get away, lost balance, and sprawled headlong, scraping veir knees and arms. Quartz arrived in a flurry of ragged breath, dust, and spraying pebbles. "Nemtori!" he shouted again. He reached down, grabbed Almond's arm, and hauled ven to veir feet.

Almond tried to twist away, to pry the gripping fingers loose. Vo could accomplish neither. "Let me go! Let me go!" vo wailed.

They continued to struggle, the one to restrain, the other to break free. Quartz demanded, "Is it true? What Gilku said? Did you go to that boy? Did he force the choice upon you and claim you?"

"Gilku said so, so it must be true!"

"Nemtori—"

"You think so too. I can see it in your face. Say it! Say it! Say it!"

Quartz let go of Almond's arm so suddenly that vo nearly fell again. Almond backed away, preparing to flee again, but hesitated when Quartz said, in a quieter voice, "No."

In the moonlight, Almond searched veir friend's face. There was pain there, to be sure, and anger—but Quartz always had that crease between his eyes. It was the desire that Almond also saw in the other's expression that was hardest to face. Vo flinched and held one arm up in front of veir body.

They stood apart, gasping. Quartz said, "I don't think he claimed you. That's not fair, to say that I think that. But, Nemtori, I also cannot know that it is not true unless you tell me." He drew in a ragged breath. "And it would break my heart, but I need to know."

Almond looked down at the rubble of rock and twig and spine at veir feet. A detached corner of veir mind noted that among the stones lay the tiny bleached skull of some desert creature. Vo brought veir eyes back up as high as vo could, almost to the other's face. Vo whispered veir answer. "No. He did not claim me."

"What did you do there then?"

"I cannot say."

Quartz stepped forward. Almond stepped back, keeping the distance between them the same. Again Quartz stepped forward and Almond stepped back. It was almost as though they were dancing. Almond turned to run, but Quartz lunged forward and grabbed veir wrist, wrapped a quick arm around and pulled ven close. He closed his eyes and pushed his lips toward Almond's lips, forcing a kiss upon ven.

Almond writhed inside the encircling arm. The heel of veir hand made blunt contact with the underside of Quartz's nose, and the young man cried out and staggered back. Almond fell to the ground again, adding new scrapes to veir already battered limbs, rose once more with a gasp and cry, and launched off into the scrub, clambering uphill with desperate energy. For an instant Quartz seemed ready to chase after once more, but he checked himself and fell to his knees. "Nemtori!" he called. "Nemtori, come back! I lost my head. I'm sorry! I'm so sorry!"

Almond was past hearing. Vo crested the low hill and dropped out of sight behind it.

Quartz remained alone, kneeling in the moon-glinting desert soil, breathing hard, holding his one hand against his bleeding nose. He hated to cry, but this time he could not help it. The tears tracked through the grime on his cheeks. In a quieter voice, no one but himself left to hear, he said again, "Nemtori, I'm sorry. Come back. I love you."

Siblings in Creation, this is the Third Teaching.

Hear now the Telling of the Three.

I am Riay. I am one of the Three. I am the essence of feminine. I am all that girl can be, all that woman can be. I am daughter, sister, wife, mother, queen. I am holy, I am divine. I embody the Dance.

You embody the Dance.

I am mother of all. I am the source of rivers and the shadow from which springs and against which shines the Light. I embody the Dance.

You embody the Dance.

For it is in me to nurture. For it is in me to take care, to give love that sustains and strengthens and keeps alive and growing all that is alive and grows. I embody the Dance.

You embody the Dance.

For I am of earth and water. For I am keeper of secrets, the heart that holds all the hurt of the world in tender devotion. I cherish, I nurse, I tend and heal. I comfort all who are buffeted by the storms of life. I embody the Dance.

Queen of the Way, sister archangel, we exalt and worship you.

I am Hefil. I am one of the Three. I am the essence of mascu-line. I am all that boy can be, all that man can be. I am son, brother, husband, father, king. I am holy, I am divine. I embody the Dance.

You embody the Dance.

I am father of all. I provide and protect, so that new life may fruit and safely enter the world. All life springs from me. From the vigor and strength that are mine, come the vigor and strength of my family and people. I am the upleap of flame and the Light that shines before the clouds. I embody the Dance.

You embody the Dance.

For by the strength of my body I wrest living from the land that all may feed and be strong. For when danger threatens, I gird myself to fight for myself and those I love and protect. I embody the Dance.

You embody the Dance.

For I am of the fire and air. I am the keeper of the seed of life. I am the strength of my people, the protector of my people. I am the master of myself and of my time. I cherish and hold close and safe all that is dear to me. I embody the Dance.

King of the Way, brother archangel, we exalt and worship you.

I am Zi-Gidau. I am one of the Three. I am the essence of human. I am all that human can be. I am child, sibling, spouse, parent, monarch. I am holy, I am divine. I embody the Dance.

You embody The Dance.

For I open my eyes to the ineffable beauty of all creation, and see and love all manifestations I find there of the Dance. For they are legion. The Dance of numbers is as the Dance of words is as the Dance of music is as the Dance of worship is as the Dance of dance is as the Dance of thought is as the Dance of Being. To witness is to inhabit is to be. I embody The Dance.

You embody The Dance.

For I gaze upon my siblings, Riay and Hefil, and see within them also the full embodiment of the Dance. Each holds within veirself the kernel of the other, a whorl of the essence of the other, such that neither can be without the other, and all three of us contain all of the Dance. We, all Three, embody The Dance.

You, all Three, embody The Dance.

For I am of none of the elements and of all the elements, in equal measure. I am the mind that sees, the heart that knows, the fish that swims in the river of time, grieving for and rejoicing in every ungraspable moment, as also likewise do my siblings, for we, all Three, embody the totality of the Dance.

Monarch of the Way, sibling archangel, we exalt and worship you and follow in your Way, as long as we breathe and think and feel and love.

Chapter 27

IN VEIR ORCHARD Sarvi defied the ban on work, trudging through the morning heat to haul water from the fortress's central cistern one basketful at a time. Vo would have preferred to fetch as much water as the trees in fact needed from the closer aqueduct, making trips back and forth with the basket-yoke. That path, however, passed out through a gate that was still guarded; and vo feared that the guard would take notice and, taking notice, would prevent, obstruct, detain, persecute, from boredom as much as from duty. Even waiting for the death of a beloved ruler could become tedious, if the waiting spun out long enough. The inhabitants of the dusty sun-drenched fortress fidgeted and sweated and complained and wreaked small havocs wherever their duties required them to remain.

The stopping of toil was meant to honor the old one dying in the tower, but, as vo made veir way through the corridors and cloisters with another basketful, Sarvi muttered under veir breath, "That is all the wrong way around." To work was the real reverence, vo knew. To work to keep alive the trees beloved of the one who would soon pass from this Earth, doubly so.

Back in the orchard, vo knelt in the meager patch of shade cast by the orchard's only apricot tree and poured water into a shored-up bowl of dirt around the trunk. From behind ven came the soft sound of a foot shifting in sand. Vo turned and looked. "Nemtori," vo said in a flat voice. It was sometimes hard to know from veir voice or face what Sarvi might be thinking or feeling.

Almond stood in the hot sun, swaying. Vo looked even thinner than usual, and indeed, vo had eaten nothing since the few mouthfuls of the interrupted meal the night before. But all the Nezel servants knew the slow labor of hunger. It was not that. Rather, it was as though the young human's face and body had been hollowed out by some vast grief, too great even for one of such whip-willow strength to endure. Smears of tears and dirt and blood marked veir face and limbs.

Almond faltered forward, drawn by the water. What had been poured had already disappeared into the thirsty ground, but perhaps a swallow or two remained in the curve of the earthenware shell inside the basket? Sarvi understood the look, the reaching hand, and wordlessly offered relief. Almond tipped the vessel to veir cracked lips and swallowed avidly. Veir swollen tongue coaxed the last drop from the rim. Vo had spent a mostly sleepless and entirely waterless night, hidden in another of veir secret desert places.

When vo at last lowered the basket, vo said quietly, "Sarvi, I have decided. I must go away."

The two habitually guarded faces studied each other. Sarvi turned back toward the tree trunk and pulled up a weed or two.

Almond went on: "Father thinks that I . . . that . . . it's too horrible to say. But he sent me away. And Quartz followed, and tried . . . tried to . . . " A choked sound, distant cousin to a sob, issued from that dry throat.

A line formed between Sarvi's eyes—the first hint of a frown, perhaps. Still vo did not speak, but Almond answered as if vo had, with rare passion. "Everyone wants something from me, and nobody asks what I want!"

At last Sarvi opened veir mouth. To offer comfort? A rebuke? Almond did not find out, because another sound interrupted—a bright metal bell, clanging out seven rapid strokes.

The two stared at each other, eyes widening. Sarvi rose to veir feet and held out an urgent hand. "Come," vo said. "We must make sure."

Together they wove among the trees to a place where they could see up to the window of the high chamber. Even as they watched, hands worked in the opening. The black cloth rippled and fell, to hang motionless in the frame of the deep window: a closed eyelid. A glimpse of a greater shroud. The long decline and the waiting alike were over. The Lady Omdyun had passed on to join the Innumerable gods of her temple.

Sarvi gripped Almond's hand tighter. "Quickly now," vo whispered. "Moments count." Indeed, a tramp of feet could be heard close by. A voice cried out. Another answered, harsh with fear or anger. There was a clash of metal against metal. Sarvi turned and pulled Almond with ven toward a certain bend in the wall. "It is best, almost always, to stay, to face danger," Sarvi whispered as they hastened.

"Yes, Sarvi."

"But in this moment, best to make ourselves scarce for a little time."

"Yes, Sarvi."

The orchard-keeper's hands felt between the stones of the wall, seeking a hidden catch. A crack opened. Together the two Nezel servants slipped through and vanished, safe for a short span while plots long plotted came at last to fruition in whatever way they might.

Chapter 28

QUARTZ BARGED IN through the door of the hut, almost shuddering it from its sheep-leather hinges. It was mid-morning of yet another breathless furnace-hot day. Since before sunrise he had been sent forth again and again to check and re-check all of Almond's secret places that he knew.

Two faces turned toward Quartz as he entered, one stormy, one stony. "Well?" demanded stormy face, Gilku Nez. "Still nothing?"

Quartz shook his head angrily. "I told you," he said. "Vo is hiding someplace we don't know. It's no use—"

"Don't tell me what is and is not of use!" barked Gilku. "I'll tell you. You're the one who is useless—"

"You dare!" shouted Loshi. Gilku turned to face her. "You dare rebuke anyone but yourself, when you know it was you who—"

"Hold your tongue, woman!" As far as Quartz knew, Gilku had never struck Loshi in anger, but now he raised a hand. Quartz leapt forward and grabbed the arm. Loshi snatched up the nearest thing to her for defense, one of her tin cooking spoons. Her eyes blazed. Gilku and Quartz tussled, grunting and swearing, then fell apart, Quartz staggering off balance to the wall, Gilku sitting down hard. He uttered a string of blasphemy and sat breathing harshly. Then his face contorted, his mouth worked, and he howled, "Nemtori, Nemtori! I did not mean what I said. I was wrong to accuse you! Come home!"

Loshi and Quartz exchanged a startled look. Neither could recall Gilku Nez ever admitting by word or action that he might have been wrong about anything. Loshi lowered her spoon a little.

Gilku struggled to rise to his feet. Quartz went to him and offered his hand. It was refused, but not in a way that signaled a return to conflict. The patriarch clearly wanted it known that he was back to his usual crustiness. Nonetheless, when Loshi reached out tentatively and touched his cheek, he allowed the gesture. "Vo will come back to us," Loshi said, "when vo is ready."

"That child," Gilku mumbled. "That child will tear my heart out."

"Nemtori is no longer a child. And you cannot make ven be what vo is not."

Gilku scowled and made for the door. "I know one or two other places," he said. "I will go look in them." The door slapped behind him.

Loshi turned to Quartz, who stepped back from the glint in her eye. "Cerach," she said sternly, "when you went after Nemtori last night, did something pass between you?"

Quartz blushed hard and looked down at his feet.

"Ah," Loshi said, "I thought as much." There was no anger in her voice, only the weariness of an open-eyed woman among her menfolk. "No wonder vo stayed away," she went on, half to herself. "My secret bird." She approached her nearly-the-same-as-son, lifted his chin, and made him meet her eyes. "You cannot make ven be what vo is not either," she said.

Quartz blushed again and opened his mouth to reply, but was interrupted by, faint and far off over the fortress wall, the tolling of a bell: seven fast clanging strokes.

Each saw in the other's face the dawning recognition of what the sound meant. They heard footsteps outside, running. Gilku burst back into the room. "The bell!" he said. "Did you hear the bell?" In other huts nearby, voices were calling, exclaiming—the noise of a hive disturbed.

Suddenly, to the surprise of the older two, Quartz laughed. They both gave him sharp looks. He laughed again and brushed his hair away from his eyes. "You find it funny?" Gilku demanded.

"No and yes," said Quartz. "I don't know. What I know is: no more waiting. And I am ready for whatever comes. I am ready for the adventure."

A few more heartbeats passed in scrutiny. Then Gilku cracked a rare grin. "A strange word, perhaps, for what now comes to pass," he said. "But it is good that you feel ready, for the adventure is upon us."

Chapter 29

IN THE GRIP of ceaseless agitation, Finch paced the regal apartment, muttering snatches of an internal storm. "I have to . . . she pressed my hand . . . when will Oreg return?" No one was there to hear. Vo had ordered it so. The latest report from the head attendant caring for veir grandmother was that it could not be long now—hours at most—before she passed through the veil. One more tile in the temple, and a young human on the cusp of adulthood left to rule, or flee, or to die at the hands of those in that place consumed by a lust the young heir neither felt nor understood: the lust for power.

Finch paused at the cabinet with many drawers and opened the one vo had shown to Almond. Vo did not notice that a ring was missing. Veir eyes were drawn to a delicate silver bracelet, a lovely filigreed band wrought so finely it seemed woven of the twigs of a living silver tree rather than crafted by human hands. It had once graced the arm of veir mother, whose face and voice both had vanished from Finch's memory.

Finch stood immobile, staring at the lovely thing. Another mood welled inside that quicksilver temperament—a wistful yearning. A subtle shift of the body, a turn of the head, a softening of the face, and it was a young woman who stood there. One hand came to neck and throat, touching in a gentle self-caress. Who else had ever offered tenderness to this secret girl? The eyelids in the soft face slid to a lower, dreamy staff. One other had offered tenderness: the servant, Almond. Vo had given comfort, down in the well-house. And there had been the magical afternoon in the changing-room, too, the only time another soul had been present for that achingly eager letting out of a deeper, truer self. Jiom nodded: a ruler remembering service rendered.

A graceful hand reached out and plucked the bracelet from the drawer. The other hand's fingers tented together to allow them to pass through the opening. The bracelet slid onto the thin wrist.

The young noble held the pretty thing up to the light from the window. Her cheeks were wet. She wept not violently, but with soft grief—grief for the old woman breathing her last breath in the high tower, and grief for herself. One last time, even as the seven bell strokes shuddered through the kiln-like air, she whispered her name, bidding it farewell: "Jiom."

Clatter and shouting erupted outside the door. Jiom took the bracelet off, put it back in its drawer, and closed it softly. She turned to face the door. From the sound, either the guard posted there was already one of Nak's men, or would soon be bested by Nak's men. The door boomed and creaked in on its hinges. The latch worked, and the door opened.

It was helmet-haired Kretsipom who entered, with a clot of hot-faced soldiers behind. The lieutenant sweated copiously, and even from across the room he stank. Out of habit, perhaps, he did a reverence, enacting the bow and hand-gestures due to a ruler from a soldier. "Lordship," he said in his hissing voice.

Finch stood with straight spine and lifted chin. "You come to betray me," vo said quietly.

The other winced. "Lordship, it will do none of us any good to have such talk. You are to come with me."

"And if I refuse?"

Reluctantly, still wincing, the Beetle shifted to one side so that Finch could see that the men behind him carried a large woolen sack.

Finch bent not even a finger's width. "I defy you."

At a gesture from their miserably perspiring commander, the men moved forward with the sack.

Chapter 30

ALMOND KNEW the need for haste, but the habit of trying to go silently was hard to break. Sarvi, behind, kept urging ven on, finally pushing with a hand. "None of your clever whisper-walking just at the moment, little nut," vo said. "Run, and never mind the noise."

The steps they were descending opened through a second secret door into a place Almond knew—a landing between two flights of the Battlemented Stair. Veir face lit with delight. Now vo understood why the landing was there! And what a cunningly hidden door, that vo had never discovered it until now. Sarvi read both revelations in Almond's face and whispered, "Yes, yes, they built well, the sheep-eaters of old. But, little nut, we must continue on. Moments count."

Knowing the way now, Nemtori outstripped veir guide, leaping down the stairs. Sarvi, favoring a stiff hip joint, puffed and groaned behind. At the bottom Almond clattered into the well-house and scanned the chamber. It was empty as always, except for the thick rope that always seemed to be there, one end of which, vo now perceived, had been knotted to a heavy iron ring set low in the wall.

Sarvi lurched in through the archway, grimacing. Vo leaned with hands on knees for a moment and fought for breath. When the orcharder straightened up again, Almond pointed at the rope—a silent question.

"Yes, that is my doing," Sarvi said. Vo walked to it, hunkered down, and began gathering the heavy loops up into veir arms. "You have heard me speak," vo said, "of the gupurt."

Almond quirked mouth and eyes to say, I stopped believing in that long ago.

Sarvi tipped veir head. "And yet my tales served their purpose, for if anyone heard a sound or saw something move in the dim, they served to explain it." Vo had hold of all the loops. Vo pushed back to standing, then turned to face the well. "And that means," vo concluded, "that in this moment when we need help, a long waiting comes to an end, and we have the help we need." Vo tossed the rope into the well. Together they watch it fall, unspooling neatly. Almond made a small sound expressing approval of Sarvi's coiling-craft, and the elder hissed a breath out of veir nose, pleased to have veir skill recognized.

Now Almond inquired with a lift of the eyebrows what or who would climb out of the abyss. Sarvi said, "Little nut, it is not the gupurt who will climb to us. We must climb down to the gupurt. And the need for hurry has not grown less in the last little while." Sarvi straddled the rope, leaned out over the lip of stone, and began to lower veirself down. Veir descent lacked grace, but vo kept grimly at it.

Several body-lengths down, vo planted sandaled feet against stone and looked up. Almond stared down at the sun-browned face, at the corded forearms clutching the rope. "Follow me down," Sarvi said through tight teeth.

Almond did as vo was told, making easier work of it.

When the light of the chamber above had diminished to a bright blob above them, Sarvi grunted, "Gently, now," and Almond understood that haste had become less important. Vo took care to stay far enough above Sarvi on the rope to avoid kicking veir hands or head. Vo felt veirself once again entering veir exquisitely aware spying state, all senses extended and tingling.

At length they came to a level place where feet could be planted safely. Sarvi let go of the rope with first one hand, then the other, shaking the strain out veir arms. Almond found a shelf with good handholds and let go of the rope altogether. Sarvi called softly into the deeper gloom below,

"Promdjuk. Promdjuk." Almond had never heard this word before, but it had the sound of an Irzemi name. Sarvi strengthened Almond's supposition by continuing in fractured, heavily accented Irzemi, "I am Sarvi. I bring other. Omdyun is died. Nak to fight."

Enthralled, Almond waited for response to this communication. None came . . . except, perhaps, the sound of a foot scraping stone, and of a sigh off in the dark.

With a gesture Sarvi instructed Almond that they were to continue down. Below their feet the real darkness began. Into the murk Sarvi descended. Almond moved to follow, and Sarvi glanced up, face tense with effort, long enough to grate, "Wait. Only a little way—you shake the rope."

Almond waited. Sarvi disappeared out of sight. The rope twisted and twitched, then relaxed free of weight again. Sarvi's voice, only a small way off in the dark, called softly, "Well now, little nut, come down."

Almond dropped down easily, and as vo cleared the final curve of stone vo saw the flame of a small lamp fluttering in the dark, illuminating two faces. Sarvi's was one, beloved knarl. The other Almond had never seen before: a gaunt face, full of folds and shadows.

As Almond accepted Sarvi's helping hand onto a broad flat ledge of rock, vo perceived that the face belonged to a tall, emaciated old Irzemi man with huge burl-knuckled hands. Vo also glimpsed behind this astonishing figure a rough tunnel leading away. They had come to a new, deeper secret place than any other Almond had ever known—and someone lived here. A deep thrill rose up in veir body, and vo gasped with the strength and joy of it.

Chapter 31

HOLDING HIS SMOKY little lamp high, the old man led Sarvi and Almond down the rough tunnel, stooping to move his great height past the low places. Almond walked upright. As veir eyes adjusted to the darkness vo could see more of what was around them. What struck ven first was that the tunnel had been worked by human hands. Vo noted marks on stones where tools had shaped them, and deposits of rubble. A rough flight of steps both set and hewn descended to a lower level. If Almond had veir sense of direction right—and vo almost never lost that—they were still under the fortress. Vo wondered if soon they would come to the underground pool from which, until the aqueduct had been built, the residents of the Desert Fortress had drawn up water.

Before they could travel so deep, though, they arrived at a door. It was small and crudely made of thin slats, but a door all the same. Their looming silent guide bent nearly double to pass through it, leading them into a chamber beyond.

It was a squalid little place, Almond saw after the lighting of another, larger lamp, furnished with little more than a sleeping pallet. It stank of slops and spoiled food, with a tang underneath of old age or sickness. Garbage lay about, and the cloth on the pallet was filthy. The chamber's inhabitant, upon closer inspection, was also far from clean. Nonetheless, he had a dignity to him. It could be seen in the measured motions of his hands and body and in the calmness of his face; and here and there Almond noted touches of greater care. The wrap, for example, that the old man wore looked nearly new. More than food, it seemed, had been lowered from time to time in those secret baskets of Sarvi's.

The old man spoke for the first time, in Irzemi. His voice was deep and rough, as though from disuse. "I cannot count the years since I enjoyed the simple pleasure of welcoming company."

"Promdjuk," Sarvi said again.

"Orchard-keeper." So, Promdjuk knew something of life above.

Sarvi pointed at Almond and continued in veir fractured Irzemi, "Here is Nemtori." Vo groped for words, then said in Nezel, "My little nut."

"My little nut," repeated Promdjuk. His Nezel sounded as rudimentary as Sarvi's Irzemi, but it was clear enough. Almond, who seldom smiled, smiled at the sweet absurdity of the moment. "Nemtori has sharp eyes, sharp mind," Sarvi went on. "Nemtori knows many secret places."

The old man smiled gently. He said, fluidly in his own tongue, "But not all of them, it would seem. Eh, 'my little nut'?"

Almond shook veir head. "No, Noble One. I did not know these passages were here until today."

"You speak our tongue, young one."

"Yes, Worshipful. Serving in the fortress, I have learned."

"Your accent is good," Promdjuk said. Almond ducked veir head at the compliment. Something about this ancient person in the dark reached through veir habitual reserve.

"Long have I kept myself to myself in these dark passages," the old man said. "Years and years, eh, Sarvi?"

"Yes."

"There are ways out. When I can bear the silence and the darkness no longer, I allow myself the pleasure of a journey back to the surface. Always at night, though, and always with great care not to be seen from the fortress."

Eo's spirit-sighting!" Almond blurted. "Were you out in a stream bed yesterday? Yesterday morning early?"

"Indeed I was," said the old man, sounding surprised. "How could you know that?"

"Eo told me. He's a servant of the castle, and a friend. He saw you."

"Ah, I see. So I faltered in my long caution. Another time, it would be a trouble that I was seen. For I was supposed to be banished, long ago. That schemer Nak Fikoreh, he whispered poison in My Lady's ear. He made her believe that I sought to supplant her, and put her son in her place. Eh, Sarvi?"

"Yes, Promdjuk."

"And once banished, if one returns, it is death to pay. So, I have lived down here ever since, with faithful old Sarvi to put provisions down the well. A good thing they built that aqueduct, eh, Sarvi?"

"Promdjuk. Time presses."

"It has been hard in some ways," the old man went on, still unhurried. He was taking pleasure, it seemed, in the unusual luxury of someone to talk to.

Almond said, "Lonely?"

"Yes, it has been lonely. But also, a solace. I think perhaps I make a better hermit than a nobleman."

A silence opened out. Promdjuk's head drooped and his eyes began to close. Sarvi coughed. The head jerked up again. "Yes," Promdjuk said. "Time presses. And at long last I can emerge once more into the daylight. I wonder how my eyes will do in the sun."

While talking the old man had hunkered down on the rock floor by his sleeping pallet. Now he planted a hand, pushed to rise, and sank back again with a grunt. Almond, struck by how frail he seemed, stepped close. Eyes level with each other's eyes, they looked into each other's faces. Almond moved closer, offering a shoulder. Vo felt the huge knobbed hand grip, and planted veir feet apart. Up close the smell of sickness was stronger, and Almond's secret heart went out, all at once, to this serene dilapidated watcher in the dark. With another grunt, leaning so heavily that Almond's knees almost buckled, Promdjuk pushed and swayed to standing once more. "Thank you, Nemtori," he said.

"It is nothing, Worshipful."

"Kindness is more than nothing."

To this Almond found no reply. Vo contented veirself with staying close, moving beside as the long legs crane-stalked along. Promdjuk extinguished the larger lamp, took up the smaller one again, and led them back out of the chamber—closing the door carefully behind—and on into further passages.

Here too could be seen the work of human hands. An unfathomable amount of time ago someone had undertaken a great labor, widening, excavating, leveling. After a long span of creeping through twisty tunnels, Promdjuk gestured to a side-passage half-glimpsed at the edge of the lamp's light and said, "Here is a store of arms and armor that may at last again be of use." At the same moment, Almond noted on the edges and faces of rock ahead the first glints of pale light. Somewhere close before them lay a way back out into the sunlit world.

Chapter 32

TWO SOLDIERS tied Finch's hands behind veir back, bound veir legs together, and stuffed a wad of wool into veir mouth. Tipped off veir feet, vo contrived as best vo could to collapse in the direction of a carpeted part of the floor. The soldiers worked the sack up from veir feet over veir head, then tied off the opening. By the smell and dust, the sack had previously been used to store millet flour. Finch did veir best to lie still and work veir mind.

Veir situation now, vo realized, was something like the game of monarchs that vo played sometimes with a tutor. In that play, once a player had the advantage, the pressure came on that player to convert that advantage to a victory. In a way, Finch had learned, this pressure offered to the one playing defense a curious freedom. If the disadvantaged player stayed strong and continued to fight, the other could sometimes become overconfident or, conversely, get rattled. Errors and tricks were still possible. For the moment, Finch had little choice or power . . . but the game was not over yet. Vo had allies. Oreg, for one. The servant Almond for another. Others besides. With no allies present at this moment, Finch determined to stay quiet, learn what vo could, and let them underestimate ven if they might.

The Beetle issued curt orders. Hands seized Finch and hoisted ven up onto shoulders. Vo closed veir eyes against the powdery sack-dust, and prepared to track as best vo could where vo was being carried. The door creaked open. They passed out into the hall. Someone at floor level uttered a heart-rending sound of agony. Evidently one guard at least had stayed loyal to the House of Z'Borforeh. Finch heard the sound of the Beetle's blade being drawn from its sheath, followed by the death-blow and a final gasp and gurgle. In pity and horror vo could not suppress a reaction, twisting in the sack, nearly causing those who carried ven to spill ven onto the floor. This earned ven a curse from the Beetle and a hard blow to the head by, it would seem, the butt of a sword. "Silence, Lordship," the captain hissed. "I am to deliver you alive, but there is much pain to be found between free and dead." Finch subsided, filing crucial information away. So, it was to be a long game, then. Vo felt a thrill, despite peril and sharp discomforts. This was as complex as the game of monarchs, with real lives and a throne in the balance.

The pommel had struck veir forehead above the eye. The spot sang with pain. Vo could feel blood oozing. These sensations, combined with the jostle of being carried, brought on a churning of the gut. Thinking how horrible it would be to empty the contents of veir stomach into the wool stuffed in veir mouth, Finch fought down the rising sickness. For a span this took all of veir concentration, and vo lost track of where vo was being taken.

After a while Finch heard footsteps. By the sound, a squad of soldiers approached. The Beetle ordered a halt. A new voice reported that several members of the Lady Omdyun's honorary guard had been killed, taken by surprise at their posts around her deathbed. Listening to this news, the young human in the sack felt a change inside. Past and present hurts merged and transformed into a stone-hard resolve. Fear became remote—a mere idea rather than a present emotion. Nak had everything to answer for now. This conflict would end with either the First Minster's death, or the young heir's.

Once the squad had been sent away, the Beetle testily ordered his men to hoist Finch up once more. The man in back, carrying the bulk of Finch's weight, appeared to be tiring. Again and again he almost dropped ven, and Finch's heart beat in veir throat as vo imagined hitting the stone floor with no way to soften the fall. The route forward included more twists and turns, and more flights of stairs, all going down. They were descending into the bowels of the fortress, the sectors Finch knew least. Vo had visited them seldom, and mostly years ago when, as a child, vo had on rare occasions been given freedom to explore.

At last Kretsipom ordered another halt, and the two soldiers dumped Finch on the floor. Vo landed hard, adding a bruised hip to veir growing catalog of hurts, but remained alert, straining with ears and other senses to learn where they were and what might happen next. There came a clanking of keys. The Beetle issued another order, and hands began working at the bound-shut mouth of the sack. Finch concentrated on slow breathing. With the gag in veir mouth, vo kept feeling the impulse to breathe faster and faster, and then veir chest began to feel tight and terror mounted until two thin nostrils were not enough.

When the sack was pulled from over veir eyes, vo saw they were in a low torchlit passage near a crooked wooden door. Before vo could hazard a guess about where they might be, footsteps announced the arrival of someone new. From where Finch lay vo could not see who it was, but then the newcomer spoke, and Finch closed veir eyes and pretended to be unconscious. Nak Fikoreh had come. Swift death might follow.

"What do you do there, you fool?" snarled the First Minister.

"As you instructed, Ruler," Kretsipom answered in his cringing voice.

"I did not instruct you to remove the sack. Now the little rodent knows where he is."

"Uncountable pardons, Ruler. Forgive me."

Finch heard the sound of, vo guessed, a staff hitting flesh, and the grunt of the underling struck who dared not cry out for fear of further abuse. "Idiot! Useless lump! Tie up the sack again, this instant!"

Rough hands complied. Finch snatched one more nose-
ful of fresher air before the return of the stifling canvas over
veir face. Vo heard the door unlocked, followed by the creaking of hinges. Vo was seized and half-lifted, half-dragged a
short distance. This new place was almost completely dark.
When the straining soldiers dumped ven, Finch's head hit
rock, hard. The impact filled the space behind veir eyelids
with piercing spangles. Vo could not keep from crying out.
This earned ven a swift kick in the stomach. Overwhelmed by
mounting agonies, Finch groaned, curled, and lay still, snort-
ing labored breath through veir nose.

"Leave it in the sack," Nak ordered. "Mount a guard outside, day and night. No one but me or those I send to go in or
out."

Kretsipom asked timidly, "Do we feed . . . "

"Silence, or I will have your own men kill you here and
now! Do as you are told and ask no more questions!"

No further words were spoken. In a flurry of scraping
feet all there except the one bound and gagged in a sack left
the room. The door shut. The lock worked. Finch, battered
but not yet broken, lay motionless in near-darkness and
silence.

Siblings in Creation, this is the Fourth Teaching.

I stood with the Three and looked upon their faces as they spoke into my mind. There was no sound but the wind in the short grass, bending and shaking the stems. The Light was that of a midsummer midnight, but if the sun was in the sky I could not have said where it was. The pale illumination shone all around us, as though the air itself burned with an unconsuming fire.

But then all was changed, for there came a singing as of myriad celestial voices. And also the Light changed; for now it was as if the sun shone down from the very zenith. Great beams struck down, and the Three lifted their arms and sang, joining their voices to the unseen choir.

Down out of the white blaze above came a great Bird. I could hardly bear to look upon it, for the Light that came from it and the uncanny beauty of its being seared my eyes and mind; but I saw feathers etched as if in silver and diamond, and a sharp bright beak, hooked like that of an eagle, and eyes full of the depths of spirals within spirals, going down and down and rising up and up forever.

I looked into the eyes of this holy Sun Bird, and I sank down and rose up through layers within layers, never ending, joining a Dance incomprehensible in its complexity, but also so simple in its rejoicing that my heart opened like a flower, laughing with delight. I let my Being dance free. I let go of who I was, or had ever been: human, angel, animal, or what have you; woman, man, child, elder, or what have you. I disappeared into the Dance as a single drop of rain into a limitless ocean, and I knew joy, and was content.

After a timeless time, returning out of a limitless realm, I felt my feet once more upon the ground. I looked down; great shining talons were there. I raised my arms and they were magnificent wings of silver and Light, unfurling high over my head. I leapt up into flight, feeling as I did an echo returning of the infinite joy I had inhabited before. And in the leaping I found myself once more in human form, in my chamber, looking out my window to the north. I saw no longer bare folds of grassy land losing themselves in far shadow, but the scene I know and love from that window, of birch forests fading into northern mist. I looked down and saw my own two feet, naked against cold stone; but I knew also with the deep unshakeable knowing of the Meaningful Dream that my metamorphosis had been real, and that whatever form I showed to the world, I was, and would remain for all the rest of my life, still also the Bird of the Sun.

In that same knowing, I knew also that I had returned from my journey endowed with a sacred trust. The Three I felt within me now, and likewise the Bird of the Sun; and Three and One together impelled me to go forth and teach that all is Three, that Three is One, that One is all, and that there is a Way for all to follow such that each new soul may choose to enact womanhood in the world, or manhood, or not either of these choices, but something between or of both or elsewise apart. Meb Netál I had become, the Sun Bird, first Keeper of Riria Dizdi, the Way, destined to show to any and all who would choose to journey with me the path to revelation, liberation, and eternal joy.

Chapter 33

ALONG THE STREET OF JEWELS clusters of garble and fret formed, shifted, broke apart, and formed anew. Rumors flew from mouth to ear, from hut to hut. The moment of crisis had come, and no agreement had been reached in the long debate in the Nezel servant community about what to do when her Ladyship finally passed on. Some hurried inside to pack a few belongings, preparing to flee, while others armed themselves as best they could in anticipation of imminent attack.

Eventually, amidst the wrangle, some at least of the community began to gather in a bare-earthed open place, halfway along the row of houses—as close as they had to a village square. One loose knot clustered around Gilku, standing with a homemade spear in his hand. Quartz stood with him, a savage light shining in his eyes. Another cluster orbited the imposing figure of Meji Kaz, who proclaimed in a carrying voice a mix of sacred invocations and reassurances to those clutching at her robes that there was still time to escape. Gilku walked toward her. His followers followed. The two clusters became one, centered around the two community leaders—an egg with two yolks.

"Revered One," Gilku rumbled, "You are our Keeper of the Way, but your counsel is not infallible. Why this craven talk of flight?"

"Did not our beloved Meb Netál say, 'Better it is to stay true in exile than to bend to the oppressor's yoke'?" Some of those behind her nodded and murmured. That was the text, that was the sacred text.

"So it was spoken," replied Gilku. He raised his voice, addressing no longer just the holy woman in front of him, but all gathered there. "But consider, my people," he called out.

"Firstly, we know not what passes behind the wall." He let silence stretch, and the ears of the assembly strained to listen. All that could be heard were the usual sounds of a hot desert morning. Wind. Insects. The raucous caw of a crow. There, what was that? A shout . . . but no more. "We know not what passes," Gilku said again. "And well it may be that what does pass will have little effect on us. What do they matter to us, the wranglings of the sheep-eaters?"

A cry came from a person standing at the edge of the crowd. "Look! Someone comes!"

All turned and looked. Not from the fortress did the figures come, but from across the inner wastes, a jumbled land of hot rocks, spiny cacti, and little else. Three figures approached, clear enough despite the heat-waver: Almond, Sarvi, and a towering emaciated Irzemi elder none there could recall having seen before.

"Nemtori!" Loshi cried, running forward to wrap her child in her arms. Almond squeezed her back. They returned together to where Gilku stood watching. Quartz was no longer with him. He had walked a few steps away and stood with his back turned and his shoulders hunched.

As Almond approached, Gilku's eyes flickered and dropped. Almond stepped forward deliberately and wrapped veir arms around him. Gilku hesitated before patting ven awkwardly between the shoulder blades. "I was worried," he said gruffly, and Almond nodded against him, accepting these words as the apology and the expression of returned love vo knew them to be.

Gilku's attention turned to the gaunt newcomer, who stood squinting uncomfortably in the morning glare. "Who is this?" he demanded.

Sarvi answered. "This is Promdjuk—a noble among the Irzemi. When he was young, he served her who now lies dead in the room behind the black curtain."

The crowd muttered, suspicious. Sarvi went on: "Our Lady Omdyun turned on him, for Nak lied to her, telling her that Promdjuk plotted to take her throne and give it while she still lived to her son, so she sent him away, never to return on pain of death. He hid instead, in the deeper passages below the well-house, and has lived there ever since—"

"The gupurt!" Quartz exclaimed. The excitement of this insight had brought his face around. "He is the gupurt!"

"Yes, yes," said Sarvi, annoyed at the interruption. "Or at least, that's what I let everyone believe—"

"And that's why you were lowering—"

"Peace, young one!" barked Gilku. Quartz scowled, but subsided. Almond caught veir friend's eye, and his expression convulsed with embarrassment and misery. He turned and walked a little way off again.

Promdjuk had leaned down stiffly to murmur in Sarvi's ear. Sarvi relayed, "Promdjuk says, we may be of different peoples, but we have the same enemy." In the crowd's murmur this time, notes of approval could be heard mixed with the continued distrust.

Meji Kaz spoke. "Worthy kinfriends, I call for Fadi." The word named a formal gathering of the community—a rare event, and only in great need. "If there ever was a time for Fadi, surely this is that time."

Faces turned to Gilku, the most likely to object. After a moment, he lowered his chin to show agreement.

Chapter 34

THE PEOPLE BUSTLED to seat themselves on the ground, forming concentric circles facing into a bare space in the middle. A few there cast dark glances at Promdjuk, who had moved away to crouch in the shade of a hut, but no one called aloud for him to be sent away. Meji Kaz called out the phrases that set the Fadi ritual going.

According to the rules of Fadi, one person at a time could rise to speak, and all present were to stay silent until vo was done. Meji Kaz, already standing, spoke first, repeating the argument for flight. Loshi stood next and implored that whatever they chose to do, they stay together as a people. Gilku seemed to feel he had already spoken enough and remained silent, but others stood and argued either for flight or for staying and fighting.

Quartz had chosen a seat as far across the circle as he could get from Almond, but if in so doing he hoped to avoid ven, he had failed, for now they could hardly help looking at each other. At first, he would not meet veir eyes. Almond kept trying to link their gazes, and finally, blushing, he returned the look. Almond remembered the rough hand, the pressing mouth, but vo kept veir face still. After a long moment, vo lifted veir eyebrows. The gesture said, "Well? Have you nothing to say?"

Quartz's mouth worked, but, slowly, his face changed. Pain came into it, and remorse. One more time his eyes almost skittered away, but then, with visible effort, his hand came up to his mouth, touched there, and turned out, fingers splayed. It was a sign from their hand-talk. It meant "I'm sorry."

Almond signed back a clenched hand opening: "All is well."

Relief came into Quartz's face, and he signed the same again, heartfelt this time. Almond signed back again, all is well, and added another gesture, not in their lexicon, but clear enough: a hand first pressed to the heart, then turned outward in the air toward him.

Quartz nodded and repeated the new gesture back.

A pause had come in the talking. Almond saw Quartz's beloved face undergo another rapid change, and had only a moment to decide not to be surprised when he scrambled to his feet.

A murmur passed around the circle. Quartz was not yet Named, and so was still, according to dictates of Riria Dizdi, a child. As such, he had no right to speak in Fadi. Before anyone could say so out loud, though, he cried out, "I am already a man!" This silenced the crowd. For a moment, only the ratchet and buzz of simmering noon could be heard. "The Naming has been put back and put back, and I would have been Named moons ago but for the fooleries of the fortress. And what I want to know is, when is the Naming to be? For if it is to come to fighting, I will fight as a man. I claim my manhood. I want my Naming!" He shot a blazing look around the circle and sat down. Almond signed love again. Cerach returned only a fiery look, but vo knew he had seen and felt.

Meji Kaz gathered herself to rise, perhaps to answer the question about Naming, but Sarvi stood first. Another murmur passed around the circle—the old orcharder was so silent so much of the time. Vo waited for hush to return before vo spoke. "Kinfriends, between instant flight and a fight to the death, there is a third path. Not a happy one, but no paths forward from here are easy, happy paths." Vo scanned around the circle. "There are few here old enough to remember, as I do, the time before our exile. In that time, step by little step, those who had taken power in our land made us less and less like them, by decree and usage, until finally in their eyes we were no longer like them at all, humans standing face to face, but like animals. Then they were able to do with us as they wished."

Here there came a whisper, there a sad shake of a head. Yes, some there remembered, or had heard the tales. Sarvi went on: "And it was our undoing . . . but, kinfriends, it took time. Did we not talk long among ourselves? Did we not plan our flight, so that, rather than being driven forth or slaughtered like mere beasts, we left our homes at the time and in the way of our own choosing? And though we now labor in servitude in a land far from home, yet we live, and we have hope of someday returning and winning back what was once ours, our freedom and our sovereignty and our feet on the Way."

Despite the custom of holding silence, a gust of exclamation, almost a cheer, rippled through the crowd.

"If Nak has seized power—and I do not see how he can have failed in his schemes—he will not slaughter us. He hates us, but he needs us. We do all almost all the work. We run the fortress. You watch: the first we will hear is, new orders. New rules. The beginning of turning us into beasts. But it takes time, and in time there is hope."

At this moment a cry called away the attention of the crowd. A child had been sent as lookout to the end of the street, in the direction of the fortress entrance. Now vo came running back, calling, "They come! Someone comes!"

The Nezel people roiled to their feet. A few hands seized makeshift weapons. There was a tense pause before, accompanied by the dust of their tramping advance, a cluster of figures came into view. There were perhaps a dozen guards, and at their head a slight form wrapped in the robe of a functionary of the house.

Almond found Quartz at veir side. They exchanged one more look, cementing their reunion. Quartz raised his hand and lowered it again, deciding against touching. Almond gave back a sad small smile: it is probably best so. Vo whispered to veir friend, "Look who leads them: heartless Lork."

"See," said Sarvi in an undertone, "even now it begins."

Chapter 35

STANDING SIDE BY SIDE with Quartz, Almond watched as several leaders of the Nezel community, Loshi, Gilku, Sarvi, and Meji Kaz among them, stepped forward to meet the advancing figures. The soldiers marched stone-faced behind the messenger they escorted. Lork, with his neatly-composed humorless face and the stiff and awkward movements of his body, seemed more like a wooden puppet than a man. All the rest stood still, watching. Almond's quick eyes caught a flurry of movement: veir mother's friend Shadlashu leading Promdjuk into veir hut, out of sight.

The sun shone nearly at the zenith, pressing down with its great unrelenting heat, and Lork's brow gleamed with perspiration, but that was the only sign of humanity about him. He stopped a few body-lengths away from the Nezel leaders facing him. For a long moment all stood, as though they were equals. Then Lork made the Irzemi hand gesture requiring deference.

The crowd swayed, but did not immediately obey. No one there had ever seen anyone but a member of the royal family make that particular gesture. Nor had it ever been made to a whole group of servants, only by one person to one or two others. Furthermore, little harmless-looking Lork had made the sign without force, almost diffidently. Should they comply? What exactly was happening?

Lork said a quiet word back over his shoulder, and the squad of soldiers advanced a pace. The Nezel in their clusters shifted forward and back, expressing in motion the debate still unresolved—to fight, or flee, or persevere and bide their time. All still stood, though. No one had lowered veirself to the earth.

Lork repeated the hand gesture, again without vehemence. Meji Kaz stepped forward and opened her mouth to speak, and in one swift motion the frontmost soldier strode forward to meet her and thrust his spear clean through her chest. The Officiant screamed, convulsed, and collapsed.

A gasp and cry erupted from the gathered Nezel, and several more of them surged forward. The soldiers stepped to meet them, and in the span of at most three heartbeats two more people had been run through. The others fell back in disarray, chaos. Some shouted and brandished weapons, but dared not advance; others lamented; some ran, they knew not where, for there was nowhere to run; and now a few knelt and put their faces in the dirt.

Almond and Quartz still stood, stunned by what they had just seen, watching their parents and Sarvi facing Lork and the soldiers. For a third time Lork made the hand signal. Sarvi said something to Gilku too faint to hear, and Gilku nodded. Both of them turned around, one to each side of the fan of people behind them.

It was Sarvi who had turned to the side Almond and Quartz stood on. Wretched of heart, Almond searched that seamed, beloved face, seeking to understand how to be and do in this moment. Vo glanced at Quartz at veir side and saw him doing the same, but with more rage and shame than Almond veirself was feeling.

For veir part, though vo was shaking and veir cheeks were wet, the response that rose up inside Almond to the senseless murders vo had just witnessed was not to lament or rage, but to stay encapsulated within self and to wait to see what to do. This could be war, or this could be worse than war, a one-sided massacre. War was the path forward that still contained hope. And that would happen only if they, the Nezel people, somehow held on to some of their strength, even in the face of such harsh exercise of power and cruelty of purpose.

So Almond felt in veir heart; and vo saw in Sarvi's face the reflection and affirmation of the same. The elder made a pressing motion in the air with veir hands, clearly a directive to kneel . . . but veir eyes glinted the same as ever. Sarvi was still Sarvi, as tough and proud as ever. Sarvi's face said, to defy now is to die. Therefore we will obey; but they will never break us.

Quartz's eyes were on Gilku, and Almond felt him tremble when he saw the man he looked up to as a father lower himself to his knees. Almond reached out and touched veir hardly-less-than-brother's arm above the severed place. He gave ven a naked, abject look. Almond returned a slow blink and a working of the mouth that said, dear boy whom I love, it has never in your life been more important that, in this moment, you remember what you have learned about the practice of patience. All around them now, their people knelt. Gilku and Loshi and Sarvi all pressed their faces in the dirt. Almond tugged gently at Quartz's arm and whispered barely above no sound at all: "Only for now."

Soldiers with bloody spears advanced toward them. No one else was still standing. Almond tugged one more time. Quartz's face writhed. With one last venomous glance at Lork, he lowered himself to his knees. Almond did the same. Together, they folded forward into the position required of them by their new masters.

Lork spoke in a colorless voice. "Vermin," he said. "Hear now the new order. The Lady Omdyun is gone to join the Uncountable Holies. My Lord Zilumek, may the Holies long protect and guide him, ascends to the Gilded Seat." Almond caught veir breath, wondering if this could possibly be true. "He has, however, in his wisdom, invoked the Rite of Deep Mourning." These words meant nothing to many there, but Almond, always interested and listening, knew: it was a tradition among the Irzemi of going into long seclusion on the death of a loved one. "For the span of a year he will stay alone in his chambers, to mark and honor the passing of his venerable grandmother." No one present believed these words, but no one dared challenge them. "During that time, Minister Nak will see to the running of the fortress, and His Lordship commands an immediate return to all work. In the waiting time much labor has been shirked. We return now to the regular rotation of duties. The following vermin are expected at their tasks from this moment forward." He began reciting a long list of names, Almond's among them.

At first, no one moved. No indication had been given that it was permissible to rise, and all feared further bloodshed. Lork interrupted his list of names to say, still in the same cold voice, "Now," and that broke the paralysis. Those named scrambled to their feet. Loshi and others hurried to the crumpled forms of the slain. Almond joined the growing group of servants summoned. Vo was surprised to see Quartz rise and do the same, though his name had not been called. As others joined the group a screen of taller figures formed in front of them, and under cover of this concealment Almond risked a whisper: "What are you doing?"

Quartz's face had transformed again. On first glance, his expression might have been taken for calm; but Almond knew that face well, and could see something else, wild and fierce, thrumming under the surface.

"Wait and see," Quartz whispered back. "I have an idea."

Chapter 36

QUARTZ, ALMOND, AND THE OTHERS named to work detail trooped behind Lork as he made his prim way back to the servants' entrance. The squad of guards followed behind. Once or twice Lork glanced back at the guards with a disapproving expression, perhaps as though thinking they could go faster, or advance in neat rows, rather than variously shuffling or stalking or stumbling through the dusty furnace of noon.

Almond wiped dry veir wet cheeks—any further mourning for those killed, especially Meji Kaz, whom vo had revered, would have to wait for another time. Keeping veir hand low, vo made the sign of inquiry to Quartz: what do you plan? Without moving his lips, Quartz whispered back, "Be ready to break when I do."

Almond nodded. Veir senses sharpened. Vo fancied vo could count the individual grains of sand under veir leathery soles. The air smelled of lizards and hot lemon trees and offal. It felt both horrific and exquisite to be alive.

Inside the gate the cavalcade jostled and fragmented. The new order was still new and awkward to all there, not only to the Nezel servants. The guards were not yet used to acting as enforcers, and even Lork, that twist of heartlessness, was still feeling his way toward the logic of the slavemaster. So, once inside, some continued forward toward the kitchens, others toward the woolworks, while others, unsure of what was wanted of them, milled about. Lork snapped out contradictory commands, not well heard by everyone. Was he addressing the Nezel servants? The guards? It was not clear. His face darkened, and he barked further confusion.

Quartz gripped Almond's arm. "Now!" he whispered, and they slipped to the side, running along a wall. Lork saw them, but at the same moment, a few of the other servants, menaced by a guard with a spear, made a half-hearted break back toward the gate. By the time they had been corralled, the two young ones had disappeared from sight.

Almond and Quartz darted through a labyrinth they knew well, until, sensing they were not pursued, they rounded a corner into an inner courtyard and leaned against a wall, gulping air. They had come to a mean little place at the back of the kitchens, out of which passed much of the refuse of the household. It stank, but the two did not mind. Catching each other's eyes, they laughed a little as they worked back toward breath enough to speak. At length Quartz gasped out, "That Lork . . . I think he must be . . . dead, and walking among us . . . " He referred to old tales, told around dwindling fires on cold nights, to make shiver those susceptible to fancy. Almond snorted. It was an apt description.

To veir alarm, someone else laughed too, and then the person stepped out of the doorway from the kitchen washroom. It was chatty Telim, Almond's carding partner. "What are you doing?" she asked with bright curiosity. "Who are you running away from?"

Almond and Quartz exchanged a frightened glance, and Almond groped in veir mind for some plausible reply. Meanwhile Telim had stepped close. "You're the boy who sweeps the temple sometimes, aren't you?" she said to Quartz. "What happened to your hand?"

Quartz tucked his gonehand behind his other arm and scowled. Almond studied Telim's face, seeing her avid curiosity, but also, maybe, something more? The shining eyes, the slightly open mouth, the way she was leaning forward, and there, reaching out her hand but then pulling it back . . . vo caught Quartz's eyes again and made a gesture with eyebrows and head that meant, "Talk to her."

It took Quartz a moment to understand, but when he did he nodded minutely. Turning back to Telim, he deliberately held his gonehand out so that they were all looking at it. "This?" he said. "You want to know how I got this?"

"Yes," said Telim, breathless, and Almond felt veir suspicions confirmed. The Irzemi girl had soft feelings for veir friend.

Quartz put a touch of swagger into his stance and said nonchalantly, "Oh, it was nothing much. It was bitten off by the gupurt."

Almond bit veir lip, fearing this was too tall a tale, but Telim's hands flew to her mouth and she gasped delightedly. "Was it truly?"

"Yes, truly."

"Did it hurt?"

"Not much."

"By the Countless, you must be very brave!"

Around the corner of the wall, a voice called. Quartz said to Telim, "They are after us. We . . . " he halted, at a loss for invention.

Almond forced veirself to speak. "We saw Nak Fikoreh come out of the lower entrance of the tower with a bloody knife."

Telim looked at Almond for the first time. "I don't believe you," she said, and Almond quailed inside, but Telim went on, "Why would he do that, when all he had to do was wait for our Lady to die on her own?" Another voice called, closer. Telim went on. "Do you bird-people think you are the only ones who don't want Nak Fikoreh to be our leader?" As she finished the question, a single guard carrying a lance rounded the corner.

Quartz and Almond exchanged another urgent look. Should they flee, risking pursuit and capture, or should they stay and brazen it out? The last sentence Telim had uttered had so flummoxed Almond that vo could make no decision. Telim's face lit up. "Silot!" she cried.

The guard who had appeared was a short stocky lad with a candid, open face. The fragments of armor he wore fitted poorly. He stopped when he saw the three, and said to Telim, "Little girl-cousin, you should not be about. The order is all hands to work, and swift punishment for any who disobey."

"I am working," Telim said. "I am in the kitchen today."

"And what about these two?"

To Almond's astonishment, Telim answered promptly, "They are in the kitchen with me. I sent them out to empty the slop buckets. They were taking too long, so I came to see that the work was done."

"Very well. Get back inside and keep out of sight, would be my advice to you. Some of the guards are spoiling for trouble, soured by the poison-words of that little toad Lork. They need only the smallest excuse, or none at all, to find someone to harry and beat, or worse."

So many surprises, one after another. Almond was so knocked off balance that vo felt unable, for once, to respond as quickly as the situation required. Completing veir amazement, it was Quartz who spoke next. Striding forward, he said urgently, "You are Silot, yes? I see you sometimes guarding down at the barge dock."

"Yes," said Silot. "I know you."

"And Telim," Quartz said, turning to her. "I am glad we met you."

Telim's cheeks darkened with blood and her eyes dropped to the ground. Despite the danger, Almond couldn't help quirking a smile.

"Listen," Quartz said. "You have shown us by what you say that you hate Nak Fikoreh, and Lork as well. We do too." He stopped to gauge reaction. Telim still stared at her feet. Silot nodded warily. "Very well. What you do not know is that Nak Fikoreh intends to imprison Lord Zilumek. Nemtori and I overheard them plotting."

"How did you hear?" Silot said, with a touch of suspicion. Perhaps he was recalling who his commanders were.

"Does it matter? We know that he is to be kept alive, at least for a little while, until Nak can finish his plot. But I have a plan that might be the end of Nak and his scheming, and the only way that plan is going to have any chance of working is if you let us go, right now, without asking us any more questions."

In the tense silence that followed, Almond could only stare open-mouthed at veir friend. Never before had vo seen him act so, controlling his temper, making lightning calculations, taking measured risks.

The two young men held each other's eyes, until at last, with a nod and a wave of his lance point, the guard Silot signaled that they should go. Quartz nodded back quick thanks, seized Almond's hand, and hurried his astonished friend away.

Chapter 37

RUNNING AGAIN, they rounded several more corners. At length Quartz stopped in an obscure weedy corner of a garden to catch breath. As soon as Almond could speak, vo gasped out, "Do I guess right where we are going?"

"That day in the storeroom, we heard the plan."

"Yes."

"So he's in there now, Zilumek is, locked up, and the Buzzard puts out false orders in his name."

"But what do you intend—"

"Wait and see."

Quartz led them on, marching purposefully as though sent on an urgent errand. Almond followed his example, and they reached the cloister without incident.

At the entrance to the sluice they paused and faced each other pretending to be in earnest talk while an Irzemi worker hurried by, looking anxious. As soon as they were alone again, Quartz got down on hands and knees and crawled into the low opening. Almond followed. They reached the crack and undertook the familiar clamber, twist, and descent. Almond realized that vo could not hear Quartz's usually audible breath. Pride bloomed in veir chest—he was practicing the silent-breathing skill vo had taught him.

When they reached the storeroom, they both moved even more carefully, in slow insect-walking fashion, watching from the deep shadows for a long spell to make sure no guards were there, and when they advanced again taking care not to make even the least sound. The faint glow from the little tunnel-window illuminated a form tied in a sack.

Quartz, in the lead, looked back and made a gesture of the head toward the motionless prisoner. Almond dipped veir chin to signal understanding. If the one they had come to rescue was startled, vo might cry out, and then guards would come, and the escapade would end in death.

Almond moved silently forward, bringing veir face within a body-length of the wrapped form. Soft as desert wind sighing over stones, vo whisper-sang, "Jiooooom."

There was no response.

"Jiooooom . . ."

The bag twitched.

"Don't make a sound," Almond murmured, still barely above breath. As fast as they could without noise, Almond and Quartz moved one to each side of the sack. Almond laid a soft hand on the canvas-draped mound of a shoulder. The bag twitched again.

Almond looked at Quartz, a question in veir face. What was his plan, exactly? Vo could see a number of paths forward from here, some more perilous than others.

Quartz leaned close. "Noble Ruler," he whispered. "I am Cerach, of the Nezel people. We are here to free you, Nemtori and I. And so that your escape may have longer to unfold, I will take your place in the sack." The most perilous way of all, then. Almond could not suppress a shudder, equal parts terror and hard wild glee. Time to hazard a hazard, then. Time to play for life or death.

Quartz began working with hand and teeth at the hard knot that closed the sack-mouth. When he had loosened it, Finch's head and torso, bruised and bloody, emerged. Almond pulled the wad of wool from the straining mouth, and the other two watched as Finch inhaled grateful lungfuls of air. Almond raised a finger to veir lips. Finch blinked to show vo understood and twisted to bring veir bound hands out into view. Almond and Quartz between them managed, with some trouble, to undo the tightly knotted cords.

When Finch was free of rope and sack, vo faced Quartz and whispered, "Cerach."

"Ruler."

"You are determined to perform this act?"

"Aye, Ruler."

"Then you shall be honored in my service forever," said Finch.

"Ruler, if I do not die, I will leave as soon as I am able to fight for freedom in my land."

Finch's face clouded. "That is as shall be seen," vo said, and put out a hand. Vo had chosen, Almond noted, the hand not usually used for this salute, which allowed Quartz to respond in kind naturally, without awkward twisting. They gripped each other's wrists.

Next followed the business, as quickly and quietly as could be managed, of putting Quartz into the sack. When he was completely inside, with only his face still showing, Almond looked down at that familiar, aggravating, beloved countenance. "It may well mean death," vo whispered.

"I know."

One more long look passed between them. Almond ended it by leaning down and kissing the other on the cheek— a chaste touch of the lips. Quartz's mouth worked, and for an instant he still looked like a boy. "In case it's farewell," Almond breathed, and Quartz nodded. Then they twisted the neck of the sack and folded it down and under, and he was lost to view.

Quartz arranged himself on the floor in an approximation of how Finch had lain before. Almond saw a difference— the position of a leg—and reached out to fix it. Quartz allowed the movement with a muffled grunt, and Almond's eyes pricked with tears. It sounded like when he turned in his sleep.

But there was no time left for sentiment. With hand motions and glinting eyes, Almond invited Finch to follow ven toward freedom.

Chapter 38

FINCH PROVED to be an agile climber, and they navigated the twisting crack without mishap. The sluice was not wide enough for two to exit at once, so Almond cautioned the young noble back. "Let me go first," vo whispered. "We have a short distance to cover in the open, and we should go when no one watches, if we can."

Almond crawled toward the semi-circular opening, bright with desert glare. As vo approached the widening field of view, vo began to move with reptilian slowness. Below a certain threshold, vo had discovered, slow even motion became unnoticeable to the inattentive watcher. Vo practiced veir art.

At first glance, the cloister seemed deserted. Counseling veirself to patience, Almond took a slow breath in and let it out. A jumble of running footsteps made itself heard. Almond shrank back down the sluice, feeling Finch shift back behind ven to make room. A flurry of sandalled feet clattered past. The sound of their passage faded back into silence once more.

For a second time Almond approached the mouth of the sluice, breathing patient breaths. Nothing stirred. Vo looked over veir shoulder to see Finch staring back at ven, eyes luminous in the gloom. "We must run to the orchard," Almond whispered. "The last stretch, we will be visible from many windows, but it cannot be helped. We must go as fast and quietly as we can, and keep the trees between us and the fortress as much as we can." Finch, veir face set and determined, nodded once.

Out into the molten shade of the cloister they passed, hurrying along the inside of the wall toward the corner that opened into Sarvi's orchard. Approaching the corner,

Almond held up a warning hand, then risked a peek. No one was there. Perhaps in the tower attendants prepared the body of Omdyun Z'Borforeh for the pyre, and perhaps elsewhere Nak's lieutenants and minions imposed harsh new order, but right where they were, all was quiet.

Almond glanced back. The two fugitives nodded at each other. This was as good a moment as any. On furtive feet they passed under the branches of the first tree, across an open space to the next, and so on down the row. There was no point in putting on a show of nonchalance. They ran for their lives.

Almond led straight on to the corner where Sarvi's secret door was hidden. Of course vo had observed the location of the switch. Vo was just about to work it when a voice called out. The two turned to see a guard advancing toward them. "Noble Ruler," the guard called, and Almond recognized him. It was the same sickly-looking soldier who had fetched ven to Finch's secret play of gowns and selves. He looked just as unwell as before.

Almond cast an alarmed glance at Finch. Ignoring it, the young ruler stepped forward to meet the advancing soldier. Veir bearing had gone rod-straight, regal. "What do you do there?" vo demanded sternly.

The guard looked confused. "Noble Ruler," he stammered. "I do as you have ordered."

Almond, watching, thought but couldn't say, you must answer quickly.

Finch did not hesitate. "Repeat the orders, so I know you carry them out correctly."

"Aye, Ruler. The orders are, no one is to move out of doors except those with assigned tasks. Weapons ready at all times. Death to anyone unable to explain their business."

"That is correct," Finch said calmly.

The soldier looked uncertainly back over his shoulder. Without a doubt, it was Nak who had issued these orders, and it was Nak's wrath he feared if he failed to carry them out correctly. He half-advanced his spear. "So, Ruler, I must ask you to . . . state your business . . . "

"Fool," Finch said icily. "The order does not apply to the royal family. Was it not stated to you so?"

"No, Ruler. Any no matter their station, it was."

"Then someone has conveyed my desires amiss, and someone will pay dearly." Almond watched without breathing or moving, trying to stay invisible. Nonetheless the guard pointed at ven with his spear. "And what about—"

Finch cut in over his voice. "Idiot! Can you not see that this servant does my bidding, under my direction? Get on with your real work, or it will go badly for you!"

The soldier grimaced and swayed. Finch took a step forward, and the guard flinched back, but still his eyes shifted with uncertainty and fear. Almond noticed movement through tree branches. Someone else had appeared at the edge of the orchard. Vo took in a sharp breath, but then sighed it out again. The figure hurrying along the wall was Eo.

Even as Almond recognized him he looked up. He stopped and stared. Almond saw his eyes widen as he recognized Zilumek. Almond made a vehement face and tipped veir head at Finch and the wavering guard, who still focused only on each other, unaware of the newcomer. Almond watched Eo's face work as he swiftly calculated. The young beinem player put his hand to his mouth and shouted, "Ho there, guard!"

Zilumek and the guard both startled and turned toward the sound.

"Guard!" Eo called again. "It is Eo, you know me, I work in the garden. Come quickly!"

The sickly soldier looked back at Finch and did not move.

"The vile vermin, the Nezel scum, they are raiding the garden!" Eo called. "They are stealing my peppers and trampling my beans! They killed a chicken! Come and help me!"

For one more moment the guard wavered. Then, with a curse, he turned away and stumbled toward Eo, who immediately hurried around a corner out of sight, beckoning for him to follow.

Almond's fingers had found the hidden switch. As soon as the guard had passed from view, vo engaged it. The door cracked open. Finch turned at the sound and moved to the portal. Surprising veirself, Almond dropped veir eyes in a gesture of respect. "I . . . well done, Ruler," vo murmured.

The look vo received in return was all hard command. "Useless lump," Finch said. "I marked his face. It will be hard duty for him when I have taken my rightful seat." Almond bowed and made way for the lordling.

Down the narrow tilted steps, through the second secret door, and down the remainder of the Battlemented Stair they passed, meeting no other person. In the well-chamber, the rope still hung down into the abyss, undisturbed. In a whisper, Almond instructed veir companion in its use and described where it led. Finch grasped the rope and began the descent. Almond allowed distance between them, then followed.

Chapter 39

IN THE LONG PASSAGE, the young ruler took charge. No hint of gentle Jiom remained, and unformed young Finch was receding too. He seemed older now, striding forward deliberately, his face a mask of thought and determination. When he spoke to Almond he did so in a quiet voice, but any hint of the possibility of equal friendship that might have been there before had disappeared, replaced by the more distant regard of one who rules for a valued servant. Almond submitted to the change without murmur, calling him "Ruler," and the young prince accepted the word as his due.

They arrived without incident at the place where dim light showed that they had come close to the exit. At the end of the last chamber they cautiously approached the small entrance, and together, after waiting for their eyes to adjust to the glare, they emerged. From the outside the opening was concealed, nothing more to the eye than a shadowy place behind a boulder in an arid ravine. No one was there.

Zilumek re-entered and squatted inside the entrance. His fingers found a bit of twig and used it to draw spirals in a drift of sand as he pondered. After a span he turned to Almond, sitting on a rock beside him, and said, "Water baskets."

"Ruler?"

"This is a good place for me to stay for the next small while," the young lord said. "But I will need water baskets, to go back in the passage and pull up water from the well. And you must bring me food." All at once it was young Finch who spoke again, even, for a flash of a moment, tender Jiom, who added in a lighter voice with more than a touch of girl-child in it, "If you can spare any, Almond, I mean."

"We will find a way."

Already it was Zilumek who spoke again, grave and firm. "Very good. It will be rewarded."

Almond felt a rush of warmth. "I ask no reward, Ruler," vo said. "It is an honor to serve you."

Other selves glimmered briefly once more in response to this, but the answer was steady: "Thank you, Nemtori. And yet you will be rewarded."

"What . . . what will you do now?" asked Almond timidly. "Stay here and not be found, yes. But what beyond that?"

"I shall depose the villain who rules in my name."

"Ruler . . . how?"

"I do not know yet. But I will do it, or die trying to do it."

Almond could think of no reply to this except to bow and touch veir forehead briefly to the ground.

"Go now," Zilumek said. "Bring me water baskets and food, if you can. And I will take counsel." He paused. "Is there one, or are there any among your people, who would be willing to take counsel with me?"

"Yes, Ruler. Old Sarvi. My father. And . . . oh!"

"Yes?"

"Only a little while since, we met . . . that is to say, the gupurt . . . " Almond stopped and took a deep breath, stood up straight, and reported as to the majordomo: "Ruler, a man was living in these tunnels. Promdjuk, he is called. He is of your people and he hates Minister Fikoreh and also wishes to overthrow him."

"This is excellent news," said Zilumek.

"And that is not all," Almond said, flustered again by further recollection. "He also told me as we passed through these ways the first time that one of the rooms, just back there, contains arms."

"Do you say so? Show me."

Back into the gloom they went, retracing their route far enough to look into the doorway in question. The dim globe of their candlelight revealed the ends of a couple of dilapidated racks on which a dozen or so each of spears and swords were arrayed. All were coated with dust, but when the young ruler swiped with a fingertip on the broad face of the closest spear-point, the metal gleamed back dully. The weapons had remained well-preserved in the dry air. He uttered a sound of satisfaction, and led the way back to the glowing entrance. He looked out for a moment, turned back to Almond, and commanded, "Bring this Promdjuk here to me as soon as may be. But best wait for night."

"Aye, Ruler."

"And bring also some few of your leaders, if they wish to come—but have a care, Nemtori, to whom you speak."

"Aye Ruler." Almond shifted toward the hot sunlight of outside.

"Attend. One more thing."

"Yes, Ruler?"

"If you can find any word of my faithful Oreg, bring it to me. You remember, he was going to help me when—"

In sudden excitement, taciturn Almond actually interrupted. "Yes! He was! Oh, if he comes back . . . " Vo faltered, then blushed and fell to the ground. "Apologies, Ruler, forgive me!"

Zilumek was not angry; was, perhaps, even amused. "Yes. If he comes back, we may have a chance. Now, go."

With a ready will, head spinning with wild possibility, Almond headed out into the afternoon heat to run the errands vo had been given.

Chapter 40

SCRAMBLING THROUGH the broken stretch of land that led back to the fortress, buzzing, driven Almond came to a cluster of boulders and surprised veirself by collapsing into the sliver of shade they cast, overcome by a sudden trembling. The image rose in veir mind, unbidden but unstoppable, of the way the limbs of poor Meji Kaz had jerked when the spear had passed through her body. Almond relived the horrified outcry of the crowd, the falling of the body onto the hot ground. Images of the other two murders pressed close behind. A wail rose up in Almond's chest. Wary of being overheard, even out here where no one ever came, vo clamped veir teeth against it. It emerged a strangled whimper.

Then for a span young Nemtori lay in the grit and scour, overcome by the enormity of all vo had witnessed this day. Such a strong pliable soul vo had, but not adamant, and just at the moment vo felt bent to the splintering point. Bodies vo had seen before, but never killing. Vo suffered through another cycle of remembering. Also heavy in veir heart was Quartz, or Cerach, since Naming or no, as far as Almond could see he had claimed his manhood. The selfless reckless bravery of what he was doing—the terrible chance and hope of it—struck deep into Almond's heart.

Veir stifled sobbing flowed a little, then ebbed. Veir fingers reached for a tree egg to work. For another small span Almond let veir mind roam in a sun-dazzled dream-wander such as vo remembered from younger, less perilous days. Veir fingers crushed the first tree egg and reached for another. This too succumbed to the pressure of the rolling. The third of a dwindling supply received easier treatment. At length Almond rose to veir feet, brushed veirself off, wiped veir face, and continued on veir mission.

The Street of Jewels was empty and quiet when Almond arrived—the emptiness and quiet not of peace, but of the weight of a heavy pressing foot. All those called to work labored under the hardening, or absent, eyes of guards becoming accustomed to their new roles and power. The rest cowered out of sight. Almond found veir mother at her little forge fire, despite the heat. A new ring was ordered, a particularly massive one, in most highly refined silver—for young Zilumek, it was said.

As was veir way, Nemtori materialized without sound at the edge of the working place, and for once Loshi did not notice. She leaned low over her work, brow furrowed, hair disheveled. As Almond watched she rubbed the back of a hand across a cheek, wiping away sweat and perhaps a tear.

"Mother," Almond whispered.

The grieving woman looked up. Her face showed deep lines of distress. Almond went to her and wrapped veir arms around veir mother's neck, and for a little time they comforted each other. Presently Loshi held her child apart from her and said, "Sweetest nut of mine, why do you not work?"

"I have so much to tell you," Almond answered, and in an urgent whisper vo laid out for veir parent the most recent developments: Zilumek free of the fortress and hiding in a cavern, asking for provisions and counsel; and Quartz— Almond hitched in veir delivery, suddenly realizing vo was about to add to veir mother's burden of sorrow—Quartz, Cerach, tucked away in a sack, playing a desperate charade with death in the balance. Vo finished veir report, and then, briefly, feeling it was for the last time, leaned into the side of an adult at least a little larger than veirself, taking comfort from her solid warm presence.

Loshi sat with head bowed. Almond sensed the thoughts and feelings flickering through her mind. Vo knew the strength of both veir parents. Gilku made more noise, but Loshi was perhaps, in the balance, stronger than her spouse. A devout woman she was, nurturing, reverent, and obsidian. By degrees her face settled into a look of grim, clear-eyed resolve.

"Very well," Loshi said at last. "Nemtori, your news brings hope. At such a cost, and only for the next small while, but hope all the same. We must waste none of the time we have. The old Irzemi courtier is hiding with Shadlashu. As soon as night falls we must take him to our young Lord."

"Yes, Mother."

"We will take water baskets, full ones, and food, as the young Lord asked." Loshi set aside her work, rose from her smithy fire, and moved inside to begin to prepare these supplies. Almond followed.

In the stifling dim of the hut, Loshi continued in an undertone, half to herself. "We must gather as we can, and we must make such plans as we can." She stopped abruptly in the middle of the floor and uttered a single sob. "Oh, my Cerach. Am I to lose you too?"

Almond thought of veir dear friend, launching with wild abandon into manhood in time of war. Vo also remembered his dream often spoken of, to go off and fight in the rebellion. Knowing Loshi also knew of Cerach's dreams, vo said softly, "Can you not see, Mother? One way or another, he is going away from us."

Loshi nodded. "You miss nothing, my sharp-eyed precious one. I believe you are right." She sighed. "Much we shall lose in a little time, now, but perhaps not all." For one more moment she stood in sad rumination, then shook herself back to life and returned to filling the basket in front of her.

Chapter 41

A BODY IN A SACK lay in the dark. For a mercy, the sack had been dumped on the rough rock floor of the coolest chamber of the fortress. The body did not move, but it lived. Other than the whisper-scratching of mice going, unconcerned, about their business in the further reaches, the only other sound in the chamber was the barely perceptible rhythm of the person inside the sack breathing—taking care, one might guess from the sound, to breathe slowly and evenly. There was not much air to be had inside those thick canvas folds.

The person in the sack had been for all of his young life a being of ceaseless energy. To stay still severely challenged such a sharply singing soul. But he remained still. He waited. He had never felt more alive, and he waited.

After an immeasurable time, the door rattled and creaked open. There came the sound of sandals treading on stone—a single pair of feet. The door clunked shut again. The lock worked. The form in the sack and the sandal-stepper were alone together.

A long silence followed. At last Nak said—for it was usurping Nak Fikoreh who had come—"Little Lord Nobody, if you attempt to feign death or swoon, you fail. I can hear you breathing. I know you hear me." Silence. "And I can tell from the smell that you lie there in your own filth."

In fact, the smell came from farther back in the cave. When he had been unable to stand it any longer, Quartz had emerged briefly to tend to his body's needs. A place where the sack pulled tight over a foot inside moved slightly. No other reply was made.

Nak grunted with satisfaction, and continued. "Listen well, Lordship. After another day and night have passed, I will come here again and you will accompany me to the battlement above the main gate, where the people of our fortress will be assembled." The word "our" was not generous or kind. It was, rather, a touch of the royal we. Nak had already begun to think of himself as king.

The foot moved again.

"We will stand together, you and I, and address the rabble. You will tell them that you find yourself unready to rule, and, desiring what is best for the land and people, you appoint me regent."

An obedient-seeming twitch, on cue. If only he who spoke could sense the powerful emotions of the one who listened; but he went on unawares, beguiled by the vision he described. "You will do and say these things, Lordship, for otherwise my man standing behind us will slip a knife between your ribs, and I will take what I want anyway, by force."

No twitch this time. The quick ire of he in the sack trembled on the edge of bursting forth. There was a charged silence. Nak reached a hand toward the sack, but then hesitated and withdrew the hand again with a shrug. He said, "If you wish to live, you will do as I say."

The only answer was another careful, deliberate twitch.

Nak turned away, went to the door, and tapped to signal the guard to open.

The prisoner in the sack returned to the task of waiting.

Another unguessable amount of time later, an Irzemi servant approached the same door bearing a jug of water and a rind of millet loaf. The guard quizzed the newcomer, receiving a quiet reply. The prisoner was to be fed, it seemed. The guard rose from where he had been sitting slouched against the wall, and unlocked the door. "Clean him up, too," he ordered, his voice tinged with contempt. "He must be made presentable for the show tomorrow, and he stinks."

The servant stepped to the sack. The guard looked on, sneering. Slowing his movements, the servant put the water jug down on the floor. He aligned the rind next to the jug with fastidious precision. He sat back on his heels and inspected his work. He switched the rind to the other side. His quick senses noted that the smell of which the guard spoke came not from the sack but from a decorous farther corner. He cleared his throat. "Your Lordship," he said softly. "I bring food and water."

The sack lay carefully still. The guard clunked his spear-butt on the floor. "Get on with it," he ordered.

The servant looked up at the guard. He knew that most of the guard's sort around the palace looked down on him, the servant, as a girlish man; hence the contempt. The two stared at each other. "Go on, I said," the guard growled.

Eo—for it was he, who had finagled his way into this duty, sweet-talking here and bargaining there—smiled at the guard. "Why do you linger?" he asked.

"To see that the task is done."

Eo's grin became broad, knowing, even flirtatious. "Are you sure that is the only reason?"

The guard's face twisted in disgust. "What do you imply, *potdjem*?"

"Nothing," said Eo, all innocence. "I just thought maybe you wanted to watch the cleaning."

The guard snarled, raised his spear, and stepped forward. The sack twitched, and the guard's eyes went wary. As far as he knew it was his lord and master in that bag, and some vestige of loyalty or awe complicated his mind. He stepped back, and the step became a retreat. "See that you do the job thoroughly," he blustered, and exited, shutting and locking the door behind him.

Chapter 42

LOSHI HAD ORDERED Almond to stay in the hut for the rest of the long afternoon, out of sight. Vo was supposed to be working in the fortress, so they couldn't run the risk of ven being noticed.

It was a simple command for a good reason, but Almond found it as difficult as any challenge vo had encountered since the beginning of the troubles. The hut felt like it had no air in at all. The ramshackle plank walls pressed in. Almond struggled to breathe, and also to resist the constant temptation to work veir way through veir last few remaining tree eggs. Vo lay on veir pallet, twitching, then moved restlessly about until vexed Loshi rebuked ven, then lay down again. Vo yearned either for the green peace of veir riverbend, or the private safety of one of veir secret places. The riverbend, most of all. Vo had seen killing, now, and the deep shock and hurt of that returned again and again. Vo felt an aching need to see that birds and trees and waving reeds, natural perfect life, still went on as always, unconcerned with and apart from the cruelty that humans inflicted on each other.

At last Gilku came home, bringing the welcome distraction of the task of explaining again all that had happened. Gilku's face shifted a shade bleaker when he heard of Quartz in the sack, but he said nothing. When Almond had finished veir recitation, vo listened as veir parents talked about what to do. The plan, when they had finished, remained the same: to go in a small group after dark to the cave where Zilumek was hidden, bringing Promdjuk and water and food, to take and give counsel. Who would be in that small group? Among the Nezel, only Gilku, Loshi, Sarvi, and Almond, it was decided. They were enough to represent the community, and meanwhile, the fewer passing over the open spaces, the better. From the fortress walls came a new sense of malevolent watchfulness.

The sun dropped behind the hills. The Nez family were making a subdued early meal when there came an unexpected but most welcome development: the door creaked softly open, and Lesru was there. Loshi stifled a cry of joy, but did not restrain herself from jumping up and wrapping him in her arms. Her eldest child returned the embrace, then exchanged similar hushed greetings with his father and younger sibling. Almond squeezed him with all veir might, grateful for the feel of hard muscles under rough-spun wool.

Lesru had arrived hungry, as usual, so they returned to their meal. As he began to eat, he glanced at his family with a curious expression on his face, a mixture of bright and fierce. "I bring news," he said.

"What news?" asked Gilku.

Lesru leaned forward and gestured for listening ears to draw close. When the four of their faces made a little diamond, nearly touching, he whispered, "I am back early as one of many. Not one, but two barges, large ones, have docked down at the quay, and they carry not wool, not timber, not goods from the coast, but fighting men from the city and from down the river. And do you know who leads them?"

In the listening faces, there was only the desire to know.

"It is the Stone. Captain Oreg, who, I know now, can speak when he must." The corner of Lesru's mouth twisted wryly. "And his voice," he said.

"Yes!" Almond blurted, and then blushed as parental eyes asked how vo could possibly know how the Irzemi enforcer's voice sounded.

But this question would have to wait for another time. Lesru went on, "When the Buzzard sent him away, Oreg says, he guessed the real purpose of the order, and, judging that Our Lady was only days from her eternal departure, he disobeyed, and went down-river seeking fighters. And now they are here."

Almond's mind was spinning. Oreg returned! With men ready to fight! Prompted by veir parents, Almond quickly told Lesru of the most recent developments at home. His face clouded at the news of Quartz risking his life in the sack, but hardened when he heard of Promdjuk's re-emergence, Zilumek's freedom, and the availability of a store of arms. "It is well," he said of this last, "for the men Oreg brings are furnished more with fighting spirit than with weapons." Hasty further plans were made. Lesru would return to the docks, teach Oreg all that he had learned, and bring him back after dark to join the deputation to Zilumek's desert hiding place. Promdjuk would be informed of the most recent developments too. And then, whatever happened next would happen. They had a fighting chance, now. Nak's hand had not yet closed cleanly on the Ring and Dagger. Strength grew to wrench them from his grasp.

Chapter 43

NAK FIKOREH SAT in the great wooden chair covered in gold leaf that was one of three symbols of power in the Desert Fortress. In front of him unfolded the turmoil of a household in disarray. Out in the hall, a line of functionaries waited, summoned at his command to learn the new ways of the fortress. In the first flush of new-seized power he had sent for them all at once to hear the new order, but he had neglected first to consider the fine points of what that order might be. He therefore did not have clear answers for the cowering figures before him. Lacking answers, he took refuge in temper and abuse. Already fearing for their lives, the miserable servants squirmed and stammered until he gave up and dismissed them with a curse.

Two figures at once entered next. The first was Lifimdi, the ancient master of the wool stores. Nak did not need Almond there to describe the old man's character to him. He was aware enough of the palace and its people to know that the wool master was of a temperament to come when summoned and to listen to orders, but then to return to his domain and to continue to do as he had always done, regardless of rule or consequences. The usurper's already rageful mood simmered a little hotter.

The other figure who entered, prim and upright, was one of the overseers, what was his name? Lork. What was he doing here? No matter. The wool master must be dealt with.

Lork looked on as Nak tried without success to extract from the ancient servant any acknowledgement of his repeated insistence that wool must be sold now, in abundance, to bring wealth into the treasury. This was not only Nak's innate greed talking. The First Minister had that morning finished an examination of the Z'Borforeh vaults and accounts. The Lady Omdyun had not been as wealthy as Nak had always assumed, not by a great deal. In the face of mild but stubborn mutterings about the low price at the moment down in the markets of the harbor city, Nak could find nothing better to do than to repeat himself louder before dismissing yet another balky pathetic underling. He glowered down from the dais as the old man shuffled out.

But, what was this? Lork was whispering in Lifimdi's ear. The wool master's hand flew to his mouth, and he cast back a frightened glance and hurried out. Lork stepped neatly forward. He performed the reverence required toward one of royal blood, then looked up impassively. Nak stared back. "What did you say to him?" he demanded.

"That if he does not send six dozen bales down-river to market in the next day, your Lordship will have him run through with a spear." Nak startled. "I think he believed me," Lork added with a smirk.

Nak leaned forward intently. "Come closer," he ordered.

Lork moved closer.

"Why would you say that I would do such a thing?"

"Noble Ruler, would you not?"

Nak sat back, brow bunched in thought. Lork waited patiently.

The door opened again, and Kretsipom, the hapless Beetle, stumbled in.

"Knock first, oaf!" Nak snarled at him.

Kretsipom collapsed face down on the floor. "I beg you in the name of the Countless holies to pardon me, Noble Ruler," came his muffled voice from the dusty stones. "There is trouble."

Nak stood. "What trouble?" he grated.

"Among the guards, Master. There was a fight in the guard room. Some said it was wrong to kill the holy woman of the Nezel scum."

"They did what?" yelled Nak.

"Lordship, if I may," said Lork. "It was at my direction. Your command came to impose order. I was the one who was sent, and that was the method I chose."

Nak lowered his body back into the Gilded Seat. "Get up!" he barked at the Beetle. "Cease your groveling!"

The hapless soldier scrambled to his feet and stood at a slovenly approximation of attention, sweating.

Nak looked back and forth between Kretsipom and Lork, who had moved a calculated distance closer to the place by the throne where a trusted advisor might stand and murmur counsel. Measuring his words out one by one, Nak addressed Kretsipom. "When you come to report tomorrow morning, bring me the names of the guards who objected to this man's command." Lork smiled. "In the meantime, you will keep order among your ranks or it is your head that will fall."

"Aye, Ruler," Kretsipom quavered, and scuttled away.

The two men left stared at each other. Nak said: "Lork, isn't it?"

"Aye, Ruler."

"Good. I have some work for you, Lork."

"Very good, Ruler." Lork stepped the last step forward, close enough so that he could lean his head and confer with his lord.

Chapter 44

AS EVENING HILL SHADOWS swept across the land, Loshi's friend Shadlashu came to the Nez family hut. Loshi rose from her hearthstone and embraced ven. "I am called to my duties in the pens," their visitor said. "The guards' eyes grow hard, and I dare not be late."

"Yes."

"And the person I have been hiding in my hut, I worry about leaving him alone."

Loshi and Almond exchanged a look. "I might know the solution," Loshi said. "Nemtori, will you—but I see that you already know what I am going to ask." Almond had leapt up with alacrity. Something to do, anything, felt better than idleness and fret.

Outside the door, Shadlashu pressed Almond's shoulder and muttered quick thanks, then hurried toward the servants' entrance. Almond made veir way along the line of huts to Shadlashu's. At the door, vo looked warily around before trying a quiet knock. It seemed wrong just to barge in. No voice answered, but there came the sound of a body shifting on a pallet. Almond took this as invitation enough and went inside.

Shadlashu lived alone much of the year—veir partner was one of those who tended sheep in the high meadows—and vo kept a neat house, the only decoration a corner shrine to the Three. All the rest was clean-swept simplicity. A light curtain hung to partition off the sleeping corner. Almond moved an edge of fabric, and, seeing eyes bright in the shafted gloom, did a small reverence, eyes and hands only. Promdjuk spoke in halting Nezel. "Small, what do here?"

"Worshipful, I speak your tongue," Almond reminded, in Irzemi.

The gaunt head bobbed, and the old man continued in his own language. "The light, it hurts my eyes. Too long I lived in the dark."

"I understand, Worshipful."

"It is a pleasure, though, to eat again of fresh food," Promdjuk said.

"Shadlashu cooks well."

"Yes. And I do enjoy the Nezel way of cooking."

"Though perhaps this particular cook uses more red pepper than some."

"Without a doubt," Promdjuk answered. "My mouth glows yet. But I find it emboldens the spirit." He smiled, and Almond, startled, smiled back. The old man was so mild, Almond had already lost the awe vo had felt on entering.

Vo came forward and sat cross-legged. "Worshipful, I bring news."

"Speak your news, Nemtori."

And so, for the fourth time that day, Almond explained to one of a growing many what the others of that growing many planned. The Irzemi elder listened quietly, and when Almond was done there was an unstrained silence. Then, as the last shreds of day outside continued to deepen toward night, Promdjuk rose with Almond's help from his pallet and ate food Shadlashu had left, sharing with Almond, who took a few bites out of politeness, though veir stomach jumped. By the time they had finished it was full dark outside.

The chosen gathering place was a great tooth of a stone at the start of the broken lands. Almond and Promdjuk made their way by moonlight, as silently as the old man could manage, to this landmark. When they reached it, they picked their way around to the side away from the fortress, and found Sarvi already there. Soon the sound of feet crunching lightly in sand reached the ears of those waiting, and Gilku and Loshi joined them. And, finally, the sound of two pairs of feet came from the direction of the river, and Lesru arrived, with, behind him, the looming form of Oreg Ardjelfinz. Even though they knew that he was now an ally, the Nezel folk there moved away as he joined the band. The long habit of fearing him was not to be lost in an instant.

The grey disks of faces in moonlight turned to Almond. Without a word vo led them back along the way vo had come in the hot noon. The rocks and earth still gave back the heat of the day, but the air had cooled to merely warm. Summer was almost done. The change of seasons was coming.

Down into a rubble-cluttered gully Almond took them, around several bends. Vo stopped at the place where inky shadow concealed the opening behind the boulder. The conspirators clustered close. In the middle of the cluster, Loshi's hands struck sparks from flint. She lit the oil lamp she had brought and gave it to Almond, who cupped veir hand around the small flame. They made their way forward once more, slipping through the narrow opening. On the other side, where the space opened out again, Almond moved in to make room for the others. Vo held the flame high, peering into the murk. The sound of Oreg squeezing his mighty bulk through the entrance came from behind.

At first there was only darkness ahead; but then came the glint of their light reflected back from a pair of eyes. The eyes advanced, and Lord Zilumek Z'Borforeh stepped into the globe of the lamp.

He did not speak, nor make any sign. In particular, he refrained from making the hand gesture requiring reverence. Nonetheless, all there knelt and prostrated themselves, the Irzemi first, Oreg and Promdjuk, followed by the Nezel. Zilumek stood motionless for one moment longer, accepting their fealty, then said quietly, "Rise." Sarvi had trouble getting to veir feet again. The young ruler gripped veir arm to help ven. He moved on to the Stone and said, "Oreg, I rejoice to see you. Now we have hope." Oreg nodded. Next Zilumek came to Promdjuk, still on his knees.

"My Lord," the old man said, and Almond noted the waver in his voice. "I have waited so very long for this day."

"Rise," Zilumek said, helping Promdjuk to do so as he said it. "We have plans to make, and time is precious."

Zilumek accepted with thanks the laden baskets Loshi handed him and led the way back across the floor to the far end of the chamber, where, on a low dais of natural stone, another large flat stone rested or had been placed. Zilumek sat down on it with as much regal authority as if the rock were the Gilded Seat itself. "All now hangs in the balance," he said. "Let us consult."

Chapter 45

PREDAWN HUSH built once more through imperceptible degrees to the hot shout of day. In the desert, animals stirred awake or made their way underground, depending on whether they inhabited day or night. Overhead vultures cut their languid spirals across the sky. The human habitations stirred also, though not in the accustomed ways. Fast must still be broken, regardless of whether or not blood would be shed on a day, so the kitchens bustled as usual. Otherwise, the fortress simmered in tense quiet. Regular work had been suspended. All inhabitants of the fortress, as well as of the lands round about, had been ordered to appear by a certain time of the morning on the stretch of level ground that lay in front of the castle gates. The time of assembly had been set for the moment when the shadow of the peak of the ridgeline reached the bottom of the fortress wall.

As the shadow crept toward its mark, a squadron of guards clattered down the stairways that led to the deep stores. Kretsipom fronted them as before. It may have been that some in the squad felt contempt for their captain, for they slouched and jostled as they marched. One in particular wore his helmet pulled low over his face and kept to the rear of the column, far from the mumbling cursing leader. "Fetch the sprig, fetch the sprig," the Beetle muttered savagely. "Bring him to the battlement. Where he will be killed, like as not. Knife in the ribs in front of all that rabble." One listening would have been hard pressed to tell if this scenario troubled the good captain at all, though the addition of "And who left to clean up the mess?" would hardly have been surprising and would have settled the matter.

They reached the prison door. The Beetle worked the lock. "Come on, Lordship," he called in his wheedling voice. "The real master of the fortress has need of you on the high wall. There is to be some theater today." He entered the low chamber, his soldiers crowding in behind him. "What, still in the sack, Lordship? Yes, I saw you move just now. I know you're alive in there. Don't want to come out, is that it? Not that I blame you. And perhaps you'll make more of a show when sliced out of the bag in the open air. Bring it!" This last was an order to the two guards in front, burly veterans of the fortress soldiery. With impassive faces they hefted the lumpy form and maneuvered it out through the narrow door. The others regrouped behind them, and they started back toward the upper reaches.

After the first turn a whisper passed swiftly back along the ranks, and the ragged line scrambled into parade order. Striding toward them down the passage was Nak Fikoreh himself, coming as at other times to make sure that his orders were carried out precisely.

The column halted and snapped to attention. Kretsipom, lost in misery, almost collided with his commander. He looked up, jumped, and stuttered, "R-R-Ruler. We, we come as you bid, bringing—" he gestured, tongue-tied, at the sack.

"Idiot!" Nak snarled. "Get the little weevil out in the open, instantly! He must seem to be in league with us. He must seem still to command!"

"Aye, Ruler, aye aye," Kretsipom babbled. The two soldiers had already dropped the sack. They wrestled with it; he who was inside resisted them. One of them cursed and drew a knife. A wordless bark came from Nak, a sharp reminder that the prisoner must remain alive. The soldier glanced up to show he had heard and understood. With deliberate care he found purchase for the tip of the blade and slit the sack open from one end to the other.

In an instant all could see that the person inside the sack was not Zilumek. It was a young Nezel man, who, in the instant they gaped, leapt to his feet and neatly plucked the knife out of the hand of the dumbfounded guard. The guard grabbed for the interloper's other hand, but there was no hand there to grab. The young man backed against the wall. Soldiers with knives and spears approached in a menacing half-circle.

Suddenly the guard who had kept his helmet low, standing now to one end of the group facing the defiant servant, unexpectedly collapsed. The point of his spear jabbed into the calf of the man standing next to him. The injured one shrieked and stumbled sideways, and the circle was broken. The servant who had been in the sack leapt through the gap and sprinted away down the passage.

"After him!" bellowed Nak. "Not you!" he added, as the slender guard scrambled to his feet. All there could now see that he was no soldier at all, but the womanish gardener, Eo, who shed his spear and ran away down the passage after the fleeing servant. Nak screamed his rage. "Go after them! Kill them both!"

The guards gave chase.

Quartz ran for his life. Unlike Almond, he did not carry in his head a map of the fortress, so he ran he knew not where. When he had a choice, he went up. It had been dark and hot and malodorous in the sack. He craved light and air. His muscles felt cramped from the long immobility. He growled in his throat, pushed through the pain, and ran on.

Toward the end of a long straight stretch of corridor he risked a glance back, and was amazed to see that only one guard pursued him—a guard, furthermore, without a spear, and oddly thin and light for a member of the fortress soldiery. Quartz had the knife he had snatched. With Lesru and other friends he had long practiced the arts of the short blade. The impulse rose in him to turn and fight. He rounded the next corner and skidded to a halt. The passage widened here into a landing, with stairs running up. He leapt to the steps, turned, and crouched on the second and third, ready for combat.

The pursuer rounded the corner too and, seeing the naked blade, pulled up short. But he was not a guard at all. It was Eo who stood there—Eo, who had fed him and offered a word of encouragement when he was in the sack after cleverly scaring away the jailer. For a few heartbeats they remained motionless, breathing hard. Then Quartz lowered his blade a little and said in Irzemi, "What are you doing?"

Back around the corner, pursuing feet clattered closer. "There is no time to say, friend sir," answered Eo in fractured Nezel. Quartz blinked at the honorific. Never in his life had a person of Eo's race treated him as an equal. He lowered his blade the rest of the way. The sound of pursuit grew louder. "If they catch you, they will kill you," Eo said.

Quartz nodded and said, "And you too, maybe."

"Maybe. But your life is forfeit, sure. Give me the knife."

For a moment, Quartz froze in indecision. In him burned still the will to engage with an enemy, any enemy; but also he saw the sense of what the other was saying, and the better chance of surviving if he accepted the help that was offered. And, maybe, the life that was offered. A life for a life. It seemed an impossible gift; but such was the moment. On the board of the game they played, lives were the pieces.

Eo stepped forward, and said steadily, "Friend sir, the knife. Is only hope."

Quartz flipped the knife in his hand and held it hilt first toward Eo, who took it. Quartz nodded once, turned, and ran.

Chapter 46

THE PURSUING GUARDS rounded the corner. They were three: Kretsipom and two others. Eo, knife in hand, backed against the wall. Quartz vaulted up the stairs. The captain was breathing hard and his face was full of blood, but he read the situation quickly. "Get him," he croaked to the guards, pointing after Quartz, and the two men stumped up the stairs. He turned to face Eo and snarled, "I will take care of this traitor myself." Having discarded his spear during the chase, he drew his knife from its sheath.

The stairs Quartz was leaping up led to a new passage he had never seen before. A door appeared to one side. He made an instant decision and lunged through it, shutting it as quietly as he could behind him. He leaned against it, gasping, then gulped in a breath to hold and listened. By the sound of it, the two guards were laboring hard as they came up the stairs, but still they came, and Quartz could not imagine they would pass without checking the door. He had only a few heartbeats to decide what to do.

He scanned the room, seeing a spartan apartment with a narrow pallet and a few neat personal effects. Someone's living quarters, it seemed. No time to wonder whose.

To fight suddenly seemed a doomed choice. There was only one other: escape. The room had a narrow window, concealed by a length of wool hung to moderate the sun. Quartz thrust aside the cloth.

He had climbed more stairs than he realized. The window looked out over a dizzying drop. At the bottom lay not an inner courtyard, but the rubbly slope that fell away from the back wall of the fortress. It was many body lengths to fall.

Quartz tottered on the precipice. His heart thwacked in his throat.

The door behind him burst open. The two guards lunged into the room. Quartz cast one last wild-eyed glance at the points of their spears wobbling madly forward to skewer him, and leapt.

***

All his life Eo had endured taunts and innuendos. The thinness of his bones, the way he turned his head, the flute of his voice, his love of music—all these traits and more had brought down on him the contempt of the menfolk of his own race. All his life they had called him weak, girlish, potdjem. Sometimes his inner fire had dimmed, and he had let their words define him for a time. But he was not weak. He carried in his frame, and in his mind and spirit too, a flexible and resilient strength.

Now, facing snarling Kretsipom, he knew that one way or another his life here in this fortress was done. He had just been named a traitor, and the punishment for treason was death. His only choice, if he lived to make it, was to flee, down the river or up the track that led to the sheepcotes in the mountains. He must start a new life somewhere else, or perhaps remain evermore on the road, earning his keep with his music. Unless of course the young lord whose escape he had aided could somehow take back power; but that possibility seemed remote.

In any case, first he had to survive the moment. Eo had never learned to fight, with a knife or any other way. In his youth he had wrestled, but then the other boys had gotten their growth while he stayed slim and reedy. More recently, he had taken to dancing. It was this training he turned to now, floating sideways toward the stairs on the balls of his feet, gliding from balance point to balance point, ready to spring in any direction.

The Beetle lunged with his knife. It found only empty air. The soldier stabbed again and again, grunting. Eo evaded each thrust. One more thrust, and the Beetle's attack had become so wanton that he stumbled forward, and Eo, sidestepping, found an opening to stick his own blade into the shoulder of the guard's knife hand. The Beetle fell back, cursing. "You cannot best me," he growled. "I outweigh you two to one and I know how to fight. Best run away again, you cowardly potdjem."

"No more running," Eo said, as best he could between hard breaths. "I will fight."

"Traitor, you will die." The Beetle thrust again with his knife. Eo turned to evade, but not quite fast enough, and the blade sliced his tunic and left a line of fire along his side. The Beetle closed with him, and they fell with the guard on top. All the breath was driven from the young servant's lungs. Each held the other's knife hand with his free hand. Kretsipom was stronger, and got his knife free first. He raised it for the death blow, even as Eo, with desperate force, used both hands to wrench his own blade free. They struck together, and both blades found their mark. The guard's weapon plunged into Eo's side. At the same moment, Eo's knife, impelled by all the weight of the heavy body on top of him, sunk deep into his adversary's chest. Kretsipom screamed, rolled sideways, and lay twitching and bleeding out his life on the stony floor.

Eo though fleetingly of Lesru's face—it appeared in his mind's eye in the act of turning away—and of his beinem, his beloved fiddle, hanging on its hook in his little bedchamber. In his mind's ear he heard the ghost of the plaintive song that, if he had the luxury of another moment, he would play one last time.

Chapter 47

AS THE HOUR for pronouncement neared, soldiers came tramping along the Street of Jewels to make sure that those who lived there would gather as ordered. When the Lady Omdyun had been alive, a servant entering at the servants' gate might have exchanged a greeting or a joke with one of these men, lounging there at his ease. That time was over. Whether or not all of them savored the role of enforcer in Nak's new order, they had no choice but to act the part. Their faces had gone blank.

Almost Almond stayed behind, willing to defy orders to look after Quartz, battered and twisted in his long fall from the castle wall. Quartz's tough facade had for once cracked, and he cried out in his pain, the tears tracking down his cheeks. His suffering wrung Almond's heart. But among harsh breaths, staring fixedly at the twig ceiling, Quartz said, "You must go. I trust no one more than you to see and say what happens." So, Almond went.

The crowd gathered on the beaten earth before the gate. The dirt floor of this place had been trampled rock hard by long years of use. It was devoid of any growing thing.

Except for an occasional quiet exchange here and there, those gathering stood still and silent, many in clusters as though seeking comfort in company. Among them appeared a number of faces and forms seldom seen at the fortress—sheepherders and barge-hands and tenders of the aqueduct, and even, here and there, a traveler from the mountains, swathed in the long wraps they wore to keep their skin from scorching in the sun. The new Master's summons had gone out far.

A phalanx of guards stood ranked in front of the gate, spears pointing at the hot blue-white sky. More soldiers stood on the battlement, and still more had been posted at intervals around the edges of the space, though not as many as would be needed to keep people from getting through if the whole crowd were to break and run at once.

The brawlers and mercenaries who had come up-river with Oreg, and who now lay hidden in buildings and crevices of the land round about, armed from Promdjuk's store, were not many; but neither were the full complement of this citadel, not yet. If it came to battle, the downtrodden might still have a fighting chance. But how could it come to battle? The gate was closed.

A horn player and a drummer appeared on the balcony. The player blew a blast on the horn. The drummer beat a tattoo. All the soldiers snapped to attention. The crowd shifted and swayed, unsure of what was expected of them, afraid of punishment for unguessable transgressions.

A group came out onto the balcony. It included more guards, as well as Lork, a tight little grimace of a smile on his face. Last came Nak Fikoreh. Almond's quick eyes noted that the First Minister wore at his hip what appeared to be the ceremonial Dagger. Had he taken also to himself a ring? Vo squinted against the glare, looking for a band of silver. There was one, on the correct finger of the correct hand. It was impossible, though, at this distance, to see precisely what sort of ring it might be. Almond did veir best to quiet the trembling of veir body, to breathe and observe.

Nak advanced to the parapet and raised a hand. The crowd fell so silent that the fitful desert breeze became the loudest sound. "People of Irzem," the usurper grated. "Know this. My Lord Zilumek, now ruler of this fortress, finds himself unfit to govern due to his youth, and has appointed me regent, to rule in his place." A rumble passed through the crowd, cut short by gestures from some of the guards—a step forward here, a spear lowered there. "In token of which, he has bequeathed to me the Ring and Dagger, sacred symbols of the noble house of Z'Borforeh." Standing at Nak's side, Lork nodded.

Someone was moving in the crowd. Necks craned. Sarvi, it was, who wove veir way forward. Some of the more fearful there shook their heads sadly, already mourning the loss of the reckless orchard-keeper.

Two soldiers at the gate advanced to meet ven, lowering their spears. Sarvi stopped, standing straight-backed and still. They stopped too, a few spear-lengths away.

"Noble master," Sarvi called up. "We wish to see our Lord and hear these words from his own mouth." Veir tone was even and respectful, and Almond, knowing what it must be costing the proud old soul to speak respectfully to this one of all other humans, marveled at it.

It was Lork who answered, in a flat voice. "It is against the tenets of Deep Mourning. My Lord is in seclusion."

In the silence that followed this pronouncement, the gusting of the ceaseless desert wind became once again the loudest sound. Almond gazed up, and it seemed to ven that vo could perceive the brightening of the sky. The moment seemed to stretch to an eternity. Whatever happened next, nothing could remain as it had been.

A new figure moved now. An Irzemi man it was, tall and skeleton-thin, shuffling forward bent with years. Unsettlement began and spread, including somewhat to the guards, who exchanged glances and a few hushed exclamations. This new figure came to stand next to Sarvi, so that they looked up together at those above the gate. Nak, staring down, faltered back a step. The newcomer called up in a quavery but clear voice, "Nak Fikoreh, you old villain, you were always a liar, and you are lying still."

Nak's mouth contorted with rage. Stepping forward again, he leaned over the parapet and barked down at the guards in front of the gate, "This ancient traitor and the vile vermin standing with him disrespect our Lord. Kill them both!"

The guards advanced obediently, but now a third figure moved forward—one of the mountain travelers, swathed even to the head in woolen robes. This new figure threw aside the wrapping that concealed his face, and the crowd gasped, for it was young Lord Zilumek who stood there. "Halt!" he ordered. High and light though his voice was, it rang with the force of command.

The two soldiers froze. A mounting noise of astonishment and sudden wild hope passed through the crowd. The soldiers at the gate and around the circle wavered and looked at each other with questioning faces. The moment of greatest fluidity had come. The drop fell to the point of the knife, to slide down one edge of the blade or the other, or perhaps to split and scatter.

Nak drew himself up to his full height, and Almond saw in his face all that vo knew of the man—the quick cold intelligence, the frightening ability to adapt instantly to new circumstances, deep rage, boundless ambition. In a voice full of menace, the First Minister thundered, "My Lord rests in his chambers. This person must therefore be an impostor. I am your master now. Do as I command: kill!"

The guards in front of Sarvi and Promdjuk exchanged glances, but did not move. A larger contingent from the gate marched reluctantly toward the young heir, who stood motionless in the middle of the square. Even as they did so, a new commotion erupted. From the buildings and the lands round about, a ragged band of fighters appeared, leaping up and running forward, armed with sword and spear. At their head, striding forward from the nearest shed where he had stayed hidden since before dawn, came Oreg Ardjelfinz, the Stone, in all his imposing hugeness.

"You heard the order!" Lork barked from the balcony. "Kill! You cowards! You are not fit to be soldiers!"

At the sight of Oreg, however, the soldiers advancing toward Zilumek stopped, and the pair of soldiers in front of Sarvi and Promdjuk shuffled back. Nak leaned over the edge of the parapet and bellowed into mounting noise. His attendants and honor guard clustered close behind. Nak opened his mouth to yell a last frantic order, but Zilumek forestalled him. "I am Zilumek, true heir to the Gilded Seat," he called out clearly. "Nak Fikoreh, you are a traitor, and for that the penalty is death."

A cheer went up. A guard at the gate swayed, lowered his spear, and knelt. Another did the same. Oreg, standing now at Zilumek's side, caught the eye of one of the soldiers standing behind Nak. He performed a complicated speaking dance of the fingers.

Nak Fikoreh clutched his side. His spasming fingers gripped above and below the knifepoint that now protruded there. Nak uttered a ragged scream. The soldier yanked the blade back out again, and the First Minister collapsed, falling out of sight on the balcony floor.

Pandemonium erupted. Almond, shaking, watched as Zilumek put his mouth close to Oreg's ear and spoke a further command. Oreg nodded, issued another silent order in the battle-sign of the Irzemi, and the same soldier moved swiftly behind Lork where he stood fuming down at the crowd. The blade struck home once more. Lork lurched and twisted his neck around, trying to see his attacker. The soldier plucked the blade free and gave a shove. Lork toppled over the parapet, landed with a heavy thud, and lay still.

Every guard outside the wall now performed reverence. Zilumek still stared calmly up. He singled out one of the attendants and, there being too much noise for speech, gestured to the gate. The command was clear: *Open—I wish to enter my rightful house and take up the mantle of rulership.*

All hastened to obey.

Prayer for the Dead

Siblings in Creation, I bid you rejoice. For as there are the Three, feminine and masculine and the third that is both and neither and in between, so also are there the Three, Darkness and Light and the third that is both and neither and in between, and also the Three, void and all and the third that is both and neither and in between.

Being both and neither and in between, we rejoice.

Siblings in Creation, however much we may love to be alive, we cannot live forever. For to do so would be to become all, and in the Dance, this cannot be. To become all is also to become void, for in the Dance each contains the other and embodies the other. Void and all are absolute, and being absolute, they cannot be the deepest essence of the Dance, but can only bound and encompass it. We cannot be the bounds of the Dance. We are the dancers of the Dance. To Dance is our joy and our worship and our fate, our blessing and our end, for all dances must end.

Dancing the Dance that must end, we rejoice.

Siblings in Creation, take heart; for if you should fear or grieve the endings of things, nonetheless may you also always rejoice, for to have danced for even a moment is always to have danced. Once alive, we have always been alive. Those who have passed from our part of the dance, whom we can no longer see or touch or hold in our arms, in one guise they have gone from us, and we have lost them; but in another guise they remain with us always. For the Dance they danced dances within us also. Among the endless spinning of spirals within spirals, when a life touches a life, the spirals intertwine, changing and combining, coming each to contain somewhat of the other, giving and receiving of eternal beauty and interbonding. All we have ever been and known and done lives forever within each other and within the Dance.

We dance, spirals within spirals within spirals, endless and forever, and we rejoice.

Chapter 48

MANY OF BOTH the Nezel and Irzemi communities lingered in the square, talking in shifting groups. Voices rose to be heard over each other. Here one group burst into raucous laughter, echoed a moment later by another. An unforeseen change had come, and the people began to savor the first taste of a new and most welcome freedom. Almond heard none of it. Vo had received Quartz's request to bring back news as a sacred obligation, and hurried back to honor it.

On arrival, Almond found veir hardly-less-than-brother on his feet, or nearly, holding onto one of the wall beams with his one hand, and standing also on one foot. The other he held gingerly in the air. His leg had twisted hard under him when he hit the slope and tumbled to its foot. The fall had punished the rest of his body too. He was covered with scrapes and bruises.

When Almond entered, veir friend gave ven a look full of fire and resolve and attempted a step on the wounded leg. His face twisted, but went instantly fierce again. He took another step, and another, putting a little more weight on the injured limb each time. Almond's heart ached for him, but vo knew better than to offer help. Quartz reached the opposite wall, clutched another beam, turned, and said, "Well? What happened?"

In brief, clear language, Almond described all that had passed: the pronouncement, the defiance of Sarvi and Promdjuk, and the swift conclusion, Nak and Lork executed—Quartz growled with approval—and young Zilumek walking with head held high into the fortress as all there prostrated themselves to their new and rightful sovereign.

When Almond finished veir telling, Quartz nodded once before beginning another crossing of the room. Already he lurched less. Indomitable will was in him, and all the energy and strength of his young body. Almond watched his progress warily. Something about the set of his face, about the way he pushed his body forward, stirred a misgiving in veir mind. Into the wild mix of hurt and sorrow and hope of the last few days, vo surmised, more sorrow was soon to come.

Quartz dropped to his pallet with his hurt leg thrust out in front of him. He probed it with his fingers and winced, then rested the back of his head against the planks and closed his eyes. His face shifted and twitched. Almond waited. After many breaths Quartz opened his eyes again and said, "I want you to help me talk to them."

Almond nodded sadly.

Quartz gestured toward the door. They both know Gilku and Loshi would be home again soon. "Help me tell them that The Naming has to happen now."

"But . . . but Meji Kaz is dead. We have no one to perform the rites."

"I know, and it's sad. But I can't even say that I can't wait any more. There is no more time. I don't want to leave without being Named, but if I have to, I will."

This was the further sorrow Almond had been expecting, so it did not come as a surprise. Still, it hurt to hear. "So," vo said, "you are going."

Quartz bit his lip and looked down. "I know," he said softly. "It is hard to say farewell." He looked up, went on firmly again. "But it's all arranged. Lesru and I are heading down to the docks as soon as I can walk again."

"Lesru too," Almond whispered. "Our poor mother. This is going to break her—"

Quartz burst out over veir words: "Don't you see, it's no good thinking about that! I am a man, and I am called to fight. Lesru feels the same." He held up his hand to show a red line on the curve of the big muscle of the thumb. "We cut hands on it, did the blood oath. The rebellion calls us both."

Almond went to Cerach and sat beside him. Inside veirself, vo felt a shifting as of great blocks of stone. If a Naming was going to happen, it was also veir time. Time to speak veir truth—to crusty difficult Gilku, to gentle nurturing Loshi, to Quartz and Lesru and Sarvi and all the people. It was time for ven to say that vo was a young human, mostly secret, tender of heart and adamant of will, and not a woman and not a man either, only and always veirself, always Nemtori, a dancer of the Dance. It was time to choose.

"I will help you," Almond said.

Chapter 49

FOR A SPAN longer the two sat in silence, breathing together. At last Almond said softly, "There is a way. I remember from the Teachings. When one Officiant . . . is gone, until another is called, if certain rituals need to be enacted, they can be, by one who knows the ways." Quartz's eyes grew bright with desire. "Sarvi could do it, I think."

The door rattled. Loshi and Gilku were home. " . . . the expression on his face," Gilku was saying as the two parents entered the hut. "I would call it one of comical surprise." He chortled. "'What's this? A point of bronze protruding from my guts? Where in the name of the Uncountable Holies could this have come from?'"

Seeing Quartz sitting up, Loshi bustled toward him, hands outstretched. "You haven't been up, have you?" she scolded. "Oh, you headstrong . . . infuriating . . . " She clapped her hands, one crisp sharp clap. Quartz ducked his head at the rebuke. But then Almond watched veir dear friend's face come up, saw the undimmed resolve in his eyes. In veir own breast, vo felt the harmonic of that resolve. Quartz pushed to his feet, and Almond rose too and stood next to him, taking his hand. This extraordinary gesture caught the attention of both parents. Loshi's hand went to her mouth.

Quartz cleared his throat. "Gilku, Loshi, honored parents," he said in a careful formal voice, "I am a man now." Gilku nodded, his face expressing quick pride. "And as a man, I have . . . I mean, Lesru and I, we . . . I wish he were here to tell you himself—"

The door banged open, and Lesru was there. "Did someone just say my name?" he asked cheerfully. "I'm here now, so no more lies." Then he took in the solemn faces, and his expression changed. "I see," he said. "We speak words now."

Loshi's eyes had gone wide and wet with tears, and Almond yearned to cross the space between, to wrap arms, to offer comfort. But vo could not, not this time. Vo had veir own share to add to the burden of revelation. An answering tear pooled at veir eye-corner and ran down veir dusty cheek.

Lesru joined the other two of the younger generation, so that they stood three in a row facing their elders. This restored Quartz's confidence, and he declared, "Lesru and I, we have made a blood pact." Lesru turned up his hand to show the twin of the crimson line on Quartz's palm. "We have sworn to return to Nezel to fight—"

A sob from Loshi interrupted. Gilku put an arm around her, in a way that somehow managed to combine compassion for her distress with a dictate to bear up. For his own part, a bright hard gleam had come into his eyes.

Quartz went on over Loshi's continued sobs, with additions from Lesru, describing travel plans. Almond could bear it no longer and went to veir mother, offering the comfort of body pressing body. Vo felt veir mother breathe in to speak, and guessed what she was going to say: "Would you leave your home and go out into the world unnamed?"

"Nemtori says Sarvi could do it," Quartz replied.

A maternal hand clutched Almond's shoulder. "What?" she said in a voice made harsh by grief. "You in on it too?"

"I don't mean to give you pain, Mother," Almond said, stung. "But I know I am right about the Naming when no Officiant can be found." Veir eyes went to Gilku's face and stayed there as vo continued, spacing the words out so each fell soft but clear into the family's listening. "And, I will undergo Naming too . . . and I will stay Nemtori forever." Vo disengaged from veir mother's encircling arm and stepped back to stand with Cerach and Lesru.

The silence that followed: was it full of thunder? All eyes were on the face of Gilku Nez, which had gone statue still. Slowly, his gaze moved from face to face among the young humans who had been so long under his tutelage and in his care. The silence stretched long. He saved Almond for last, and Almond forced veirself to stand tall, to put veir shoulders back, veir chin up, and to look back unwaveringly for as long as vo could—the span of three heartbeats. Then veir eyes dropped. Not in consternation, though. It was just as long as vo could look at one time out of the windows of such a private soul.

When Gilku spoke, it was to his beloved, looking into her tear-streaked face so close to his own. "It seems, my precious one," he said, and then something happened none there could recall hearing before: his voice cracked. He cleared his throat and resumed in a roughened tone. "It seems, my precious one, that all in a rush, on a day of many great changes, we find our children also grown." He turned back to the three still standing united and said, "You are right. It is long past time for the Naming. Let us find Sarvi."

Chapter 50

WITH AN OFFICIANT present the Naming would have
included many additions of pomp: a ceremonial procession,
singing and prayer, the recitation of the Dream of the Three
and of other words of Meb Netál, the Sun Bird, charismatic
founder of Riria Dizdi, the Way. In the absence of an Officiant
the ceremony was reduced to its essential elements, but even
so, much preparation was required. All would dress in their
ritual finest, save for those being Named, who would wear
simple shifts of thin white wool. And there would be feasting
and celebration after. On this point there was no question in
anyone's mind.

Another crucial element of the ceremony was the Calling
of the People. Criers were sent out through the community
and round about, in all the directions of the iron, to call in a
lilting singsong the Words of Summoning. "It is the time of
Riria Dizdi! By Meb Netál you are summoned. Under the eyes
and under the protection of the Three you are summoned.
Come witness! Those among us who stand on the threshold
of full life, at the hour appointed, they choose and claim their
names and selves. It is the time of Riria Dizdi. Come bear witness!"

The hour arrived. The community assembled on the
meeting ground, sitting, as in Fadi, in concentric circles with
an empty space in the middle. The noise of the crowd drifted
down to hush. Some bowed their heads, words of devotion on
their silently moving lips. They awaited the formal entrance
of Sarvi, draped in the Officiant's robe, and of those to be
Named, Quartz and Almond and two others, who, with parents, stood out of sight behind the nearest hut.

Just as the ceremony was about to begin a disturbance grew from one edge of the assembly and passed through to the other. Someone was approaching. Eyes peered, voices rose. The figure who came, walking alone, was their new ruler, Zilumek. He wore not the regalia of his rank, but clothes such as in his culture a young noble might wear to worship the Uncountable Holies in their temple.

Confusion erupted. Some rose to their feet. Others prostrated themselves. Still others called out fragments of distress and debate. The commotion drew Sarvi and the rest of those waiting out into the open.

Zilumek stopped at the edge of the meeting ground. Looking across, he addressed Sarvi. "Revered One," he said, in Nezel, in the careful way of someone repeating memorized syllables. This silenced the crowd. He went on in his own language. "I do not wish to impose—and, please, good people, be at your ease—but may I . . . if you will permit, I would be honored to attend your ceremony."

Clear in Almond's mind rose the image of a dusty chamber full of feminine finery, and of the secret molten joy that vo had felt there once with and on behalf of the human who stood before them. Vo touched Sarvi's arm. The orchard-keeper looked down. "May I ask it?" Almond said. "As one of those to be Named?" Sarvi's expression remained grave and doubtful. "There is a reason I cannot say," Almond said. "But I do ask it."

Sarvi looked around at the other faces of those gathered to enact the ritual. They expressed back to ven various shades of resistance, acceptance, or disinterest. "Very well," Sarvi said. "You are welcome, Noble Ruler." Zilumek nodded dignified thanks and sat cross-legged in the outmost circle. The Nezel people near him shifted, clearing a space around him, but then turned away, accepting or at least tolerating his presence.

Sarvi, already out in the open, elected not to return to concealment, making veir way instead among the seated figures to the center of the gathering. Waiting for the signal to follow, Almond glanced once more out to where Zilumek sat motionless, then beckoned veir mother's ear down to veir mouth and whispered a request. Loshi whispered back an acknowledgement.

It was time to enter the circle. Even in this simple version of the ceremony there were many words, long incantations. The moments of Naming themselves, though, when they finally come, were brief and simple. The other two to be Named went first. Then it was Quartz's turn. When called, he limped to join Sarvi in the middle of the circle. Gilku and Loshi stood close by. As required by the ritual, Quartz turned around slowly to see and be seen by all present, then knelt in front of Sarvi, working to arrange his wounded leg.

"It is the moment ordained," Sarvi intoned for the third time that day. "Young human, are you ready to grow into the full flower of your humanity?"

"I am ready," Quartz said. He was following the script, but Almond could hear also the pure natural fervor ringing in his voice.

"Who is it you have been until now, among us?"

"I have been Felshad."

"A child in the Way, an unformed being growing to this moment."

"Yes, Officiant."

"Observing, learning, coming to know the paths that open before all of our feet."

"Yes, Officiant."

"Until now, on one path you have walked. But now the path splits into three, and you must choose."

"Yes, Officiant."

"What way do you choose, young human who until this day has been Felshad?"

Almond, watching, felt tears rising up, and let them find expression in veir eyes and face and form. Such a moment came only once in a life: a step forward. A choice for the rest of days. Felshad, Quartz, was gone. Childhood was done. All would be different now.

Quartz, too, seemed to need a moment for emotion. Staring up at Sarvi's face he swayed on his knees, then found stillness again. "I choose the way of Hefil," he called out clearly. This came as no surprise to anyone there, but still a murmur of approval passed through the crowd.

"And what name will you carry on the path you have chosen?" Sarvi asked.

"Officiant, I am Cerach." Cerach's voice was quiet, but it thrummed with hot glory.

"Rise, Cerach, in the name of Meb Netál, and of the Three, and greet your people."

Cerach pushed to his feet and turned all the way around again, to see and be seen by all there. Cheers broke out, the people beating their hands on their knees in applause. The young man's solemn composure cracked, and he suddenly whooped and broke into a grinning, hobbling dance of pure celebration. The crowd laughed, sharing his happiness, and many voices called out words of welcome and love.

Cerach sat down in the innermost row, and it was Almond's turn. As in a dream vo repeated the ritual responses, until the question came. "What way do you choose, young human who until this day has been Nemtori?"

Now that the moment had finally arrived, vo knew that there had never been any question. Still, vo took time to answer. Three slow breaths vo took, in and out, feeling how ever since vo could remember vo had felt pressured from outside to make a choice between what had been, until the teachings of Meb Netál, two and only two distinct and narrow paths. It had been so hard in the face of such pressure to feel sure of who vo really was...but vo knew now, with the unshakeable strength of a truth of self fully felt and perceived. Vo was not a woman nor a man. Vo was a fluid human. Vo inhabited a middle space and found completeness of self in refraining evermore from choosing either of the ends that encompassed it. In veir own human way, vo embodied the greater knowing and seeing and being that was every and all, ineffable, holy, perfect: the Dance.

"I choose the way of Zi-Gidau," vo said, quietly, but steady and clear.

"And what name will you carry on the path you have chosen?"

"Officiant, I am as I have been. I remain and will remain Nemtori for as long as I shall live."

"Rise, Nemtori, in the name of Meb Netál, and of the Three, and greet your people."

Chapter 51

AT THE END of the ceremony, after a long embrace for each of her grown children, Loshi slipped away down the Street of Jewels to the hut of the Nez family. When she returned, she found Nemtori and put something into veir hand—the response to veir whispered request before the rite began. Almond squeezed veir mother's hand and went in search of the one vo sought. On the way vo paused to extract Cerach from a group of happy celebrants making much of him. At first he was annoyed to be pulled away, but when Almond said, "I need you to come with me," he gave his sibling's face a close look and followed.

Zilumek stood a little apart, watching the joyous hubbub, his face a mask. The community had evidently decided that the best way to cope with his odd presence there was to ignore him. No one spoke to him, nor acknowledged his existence in any way. He was just turning to walk back to the fortress he ruled when a gentle voice calling low stopped him again. He turned back.

In a patch of desert, under a sky just beginning to become less furnace-like as the earth continued its inevitable tilt away from the sun, three new-minted grown humans met and stood in a triangle. Each looked at each. Zilumek broke the tableau first. He faced Cerach and, surveying the many visible marks still on him from his ordeal and fall, said, "I owe you my life."

Cerach bowed.

"And I ask again, what reward would you have for your faithful service?"

Almond watched the two humans in front of ven, sensing the strength and will and edge of each. Vo felt a qualm. Was a sweet moment of joy about to sour? Veir eyes flicked back and forth as vo silently begged each of them to find a way.

Cerach's lips twitched as he considered and discarded words to say. Presently he straightened his back and said, "Noble Ruler, I ask no reward except one."

"Name it."

"I have said it before. I am called to return to my land and fight for its freedom."

No answer.

"I have sworn a blood oath to go."

Again no answer.

"So, Noble Ruler, I ask your blessing to leave this place, to leave your service forever, and to go and do as I am called."

A long silence followed this request. Fitful desert wind blew garments and hair. The two stared at each other. Zilumek looked away first. He cleared his throat. "I too know what it is to be called," he said softly. "Go, with my blessing and thanks."

Cerach performed a standing salute and moved back a step. Zilumek's attention turned to Almond.

Almond started to kneel, but Zilumek held out a hand to stop ven. He said, "To you, also, I owe my life."

Almond looked down at veir feet.

"What reward would you name?"

"None, Noble Ruler."

Zilumek made a sound of annoyance. "What will you do, then? Do you go with Cerach your kinsman to the wars of your homeland?"

"No, Ruler."

"What then?"

Almond gestured at the landscape about them. "This is where my people are," vo said. "This is where I live. Therefore, I will stay and serve, as I have always done."

"And is there nothing—" Zilumek's voice cut off. "Very well," he said, in a more distant tone. "I will give the matter some thought, and then I will have, perhaps, words to say."

Almond had no answer to this.

"The ceremony of the Ring and Dagger is tomorrow," Zilumek went on, still cool and formal. "I require you to be there."

"Aye, Ruler."

"Now, I must return."

"Aye, Ruler."

Zilumek turned away and, with slow tread and erect bearing, began walking back to the fortress. Almond watched him go, then jolted into motion, running after him and calling, "Ruler, wait!"

The other stopped and turned back around. Almond rejoined him, breathing harder than the short run warranted, discomposed. "I almost forgot," vo said, and vo extended a hand holding something—by the careful pursing of the fingertips around it, something small and heavy.

Looking puzzled, Zilumek held out a receiving hand. Gently, with a touch of reverence, Almond placed veir gift in the other's open palm.

It was the heavy silver ring Almond had pilfered from the little drawer in the cabinet of the young royal's chamber. Its outside surface looked the same as before, except that Loshi had buffed away the tarnish, so that it shone. The inside surface, though, had changed more substantially. At Almond's request, Loshi had inscribed around the ring's inner surface a narrow band of the delicate swirls and curlicues traditionally reserved for a queen of the Irzemi people.

A long look went between the two young humans. Almond's eyes refrained respectfully from prying. Nonetheless, for one brief moment, vo saw a subtle change in the returning gaze. For a moment a lost woman who could never now speak her name looked out, then flickered away.

Zilumek's mouth trembled, then firmed again. He inclined his head, turned, and continued his slow determined walk along the path he had chosen.

Almond watched until he entered the gate and disappeared. Then, heart and mind and soul all full, but with no words to say, vo left the celebration. Vo knew vo would be required soon at the feasting, but first, vo needed a span of time alone. On swift feet vo made veir way toward the green bend of the river, with its hush, and whispering cattails, and sometimes one white bird stalking along the fringe of the reeds; where aside from the wind in the leaves the loudest sound was the eternal whisper of the river always flowing, unhurried but never stopping, down to the mystery of the sea.

Chapter 52

ALMOND OPENED VEIR EYES into the first moment of waking, when a self remembers nothing and only is. Had a sound woken ven? From the grey light, the sun had not yet crested the horizon beyond the hills, let alone the hills themselves. It was Loshi's work time. On other mornings, the sound would have been the clink of her hammer. It was not a clink, though, that vo had heard. It was low voices.

And with that, memory came flooding back. Vo was Named now, an adult in the Nezel community. Vo had chosen veir path. And, vo was summoned today to the coronation to hear veir fate. In veir mind vo saw the face of Zilumek, who, having taken up the cloak of power, now wore it with natural authority. He had put on majesty, and become remote. Almond knew his power over veir life, and felt certain of no outcome, whether reward or punishment, work or exile.

Again voices murmured on the edge of hearing. Almond rose on an elbow. The sound came from behind the hut. Vo rose to investigate and saw that Quartz's pallet was empty.

Vo knew immediately—and with certainty—what this meant. Veir same-as-brother was gone. And that meant just as certainly that Lesru, veir blood brother, was also gone. They had left to fight in the rebellion. Even this instant they journeyed down the river in the hold of a wool barge, or hiked along the riverbank, down the straggle of trail beyond the green bend.

Almond pressed veir eyes gently shut. Two tears ran down, one on each cheek. On silent feet vo padded out to join veir mother where she sat by her little fire pit, ashy and cold this morning.

The other person there was Loshi's friend Shadlashu, who sat close to her, holding her hand. Loshi's face was streaked with tears. Almond went to her, but then hesitated. Yesterday vo would have leaned close, burrowed in, but vo was not a child anymore. A shadow crossed veir face. After a moment of thought, vo sat cross-legged close to veir mother and rested a gentle hand on her knee.

Loshi looked up at the touch. "Nemtori," she said, just above a whisper. "My dear."

"Mother."

Loshi lifted an object she held in her hand. It was one of the flat stones from the big firepit inside, dark with soot. Three symbols had been carefully engraved on it by some sharp implement, rough but readable: a fist, a heart, and the triangle within a triangle that was the holy emblem of the Three, and that was also the national sign of the old country of Nezel before the coup and exile. Almond understood the signs. This was the farewell of he who had been Quartz, now a young man named Cerach launched into the manhood he had chosen.

"So much loss," Loshi whispered. "My two sons gone all in one morning, and Meji Kaz, and others here in the Street of Jewels, and the Lady too." Nemtori nodded and blinked, and another tear tracked down.

Suddenly Loshi twisted toward Almond, taking veir face in both hands, pulling it close to her own. She whispered fiercely, "Nemtori! Tell me, last of mine, that you are not leaving too."

Steadily holding veir mother's gaze, Almond said, "I am not leaving."

"Swear to me."

Almond faltered. "There is only this. I am ordered to the coronation. Last night, Finch, I mean Lord Zilumek, when I gave him the ring, he commanded me to come. But he is changed, and I do not know what he will say."

Loshi pondered this new information. "Surely it will not be punishment. You did him a great service."

"Yes. But he is ruler now, and I must do as he says. Other than that, I will stay. This is my home—the only one I have ever known."

Loshi nodded sadly. "But perhaps not forever."

"Mother?'

"Who is to say what the future will bring? We may yet see and be with our dear Lesru and Cerach again."

"What do you mean?"

"Your father and I, we have spoken more than once about the possibility of following them one day."

"Of going back to Nezel?"

"Yes. Or closer to it, at least. Close enough to be of some help to those who fight to regain our homeland."

Almond found veirself with no words to say. Veir mother touched veir shoulder. "Does that idea upset you?" she asked gently.

"Yes . . . no . . . Mother, I do not know," Almond stammered. Vo pondered before continuing. "It's strange. In one way, my heart leaps up at the thought. To go home! To see the land I have never known. That would be a great joy." Loshi smiled. "But, also," Almond went on, "I don't think . . . I mean, it is not all bad here. There are parts of this life that I find . . . not too awful to bear."

"It feels like home to you."

"Yes, Mother."

Loshi nodded thoughtfully. "Once you have lost a home and made another home elsewhere, there must be a loss. We can only live in one home at a time."

Chapter 53

ZILUMEK HAD WASTED NO TIME in demonstrating his intention, through open gates and other unprecedented gestures, to conduct himself in novel ways as he took up the Ring and Dagger. Protocol had become rigid during Omdyun's long reign, so there was a good deal of grumbling among his subjects, and when it became known that an invitation had been issued to the Nezel community to send representatives to the coronation, outright arguments erupted between, on the one hand, those most comfortable with how things had been before, and on the other by those most excited by the possibility of change.

The invitation to the ceremony, delivered by an Irzemi messenger visibly struggling to be polite, for once completely silenced Gilku Nez. When he could speak again, he stiffly stated his intention to attend, along with Loshi and Sarvi. He even managed to observe the forms of courtesy and send regards and respect back to the new ruler. Almond waited a span for veir father to calm down again after this encounter, and then reminded him that Zilumek had required veir presence as well. "So be it," Gilku said simply.

As the appointed hour approached, those attending the ceremony made their way to the great hall, dressed in their finest. The hall had high windows in both walls and was empty of furniture except for the Gilded Seat on its dais at the end opposite the big double doors. Those summoned filed in and stood in ranks along the side walls. The doors were closed. There followed a fidgety, suspenseful pause. Then, with a sounding of horns and drums, the doors were flung open again, and a ceremonial procession entered.

The line of Irzemi making their way up the central aisle included Oreg, wearing now the insignia of captain of the guard; Promdjuk, carrying a small chest containing, as everyone there knew, the Ring and Dagger; and then a squad of soldiers, various officials of the household, and the priestess of the temple. Lastly, a little apart at the end of the line, Zilumek Z'Borforeh stalked haughtily in, dressed all in deep blues and greens—the rarest and most expensive dyes of all.

There followed much ceremonial speech. Almond felt Loshi and Gilku next to ven, practicing patience each in veir own way. Loshi's breath deepened and slowed, and when Almond glanced vo saw that she had her eyes closed. Gilku shifted and muttered, shifted and muttered.

At last all the words had been spoken. Zilumek knelt. Promdjuk opened the ornate box and took from it the ancient Dagger. He held it high and in his cracked old voice sang ritual phrases in a form of the Irzemi language so ancient that few even of the native speakers there knew what they meant. He handed the Dagger, hilt first, to Zilumek, who, with a ritual flourish, slid it into the scabbard already hanging from the sash around his waist.

Promdjuk reached into the chest again, and Almond shifted so vo could see clearly. Was it the ring vo had given? Vo was too far away to be able to tell for sure, but it looked the same; and Almond noted that when the old man of the caves raised the glinting trinket aloft and sang again, he held it in such a way that his big thumb and forefinger met in the center of the circlet, obscuring the inner surface of the band.

The singing ended. Promdjuk placed the ring in Zilumek's waiting palm. Zilumek closed his hand around it, brought his hands together, slipped the ring onto the required finger, and lifted his hand high so that all could see. Did his eyes for an instant cut to Almond, halfway down the hall? It might have been so, but it was impossible to know for sure.

Zilumek turned to face the Gilded Seat, the third and final symbol of Irzemi rulership. A deep hush descended. The drums beat a sudden rat-a-tat, causing some spectators to jump or utter stifled exclamations. And, ultimately, the simple meaningful gesture: Zilumek marched up onto the dais, turned, surveyed the silent crowd once more, and took his seat.

The drummers repeated the tattoo, with the addition this time of a flourish of horns, and cheering erupted within the hall, to be echoed a moment later by a fainter cheer from out where those not bidden to the ceremony watched for the Z'Borforeh banner to unfurl on the high tower.

And yet the ceremony was not over. The ancient protocols required that many swearings of allegiance should now take place, and it came as no surprise to anyone that Zilumek had chosen to keep this tradition. One by one the various courtiers and worthies and officials of the Desert Fortress and surrounding lands knelt and pledged loyalty, with more or less fervor and sincerity, to their new prince.

Almond watched in mounting trepidation. It was clear that an order of approaching the seat had been set and communicated to those waiting. They clustered in a loose line, waiting for the majordomo to call their names. Almond had received no direction beyond the order to attend. Vo chewed veir lip. Veir fingers sought a tree egg to press and roll.

At long last it seemed that everyone pre-ordained to approach had done so. An uncertain shuffling built in the room. Zilumek still sat, regal, on the Gilded Seat. He waited until the room had settled once more to wary silence, then called out, "Let the one named Nemtori come forward."

Almond took a shuddery breath, tucked the tree egg away, and walked toward the dais, shoulders back, chin lifted. The crowd made way, murmuring. A short distance from the Gilded Seat, vo prostrated veirself before Zilumek. "Rise," the young ruler commanded, and Almond stood to face the throne. Vo hardly dared look up. The other's expression was utterly inscrutable.

Instead of speaking to Almond directly, Zilumek raised his voice and addressed the assembly. "None here know the full tale of what has passed in the last three days," he said. "But you may take me at my word when I say that Nak Fikoreh would be sitting here, closing his cruel fist around you now, and I would be dead, but for the aid given by this person before me, and others among the Nezel servants in this place." A mutter, not entirely friendly, traveled around the room. More than a few there were used to thinking of the Nezel people as slaves.

Zilumek ignored the sound. "Nemtori, you have been Named."

"Aye, Noble Ruler."

"And you have chosen the middle way of the people of your race, and come into your majority as neither woman nor man."

Another gust of muttering. Almond swallowed and whispered, "Aye, Noble Ruler."

Zilumek sat unspeaking for a moment. Almond risked another glance. The young lord stared intently back. The fingers of his right hand touched the ring on his left, spinning it on its finger. Once again, he raised his voice to address the multitude. "By our law and custom, those Nezel who choose the middle path of their Way are deemed base and unclean. So has it always been." This time the crowd's reaction carried notes of approval, but Zilumek was not finished. "So has it always been," he repeated. "But today is the beginning of a new time, with a new rule. And in my house," vo said, spacing the words out, making them ring with authority, "in my house, while much will stay as it has been, much will also change."

Dead silence fell. A motion to the side of the dais drew all eyes: Oreg Ardjelfinz had stepped forward. Zilumek rose to his feet and finished his proclamation. "Let it be therefore known and ordered," he intoned, "That I owe this honored servant my life, and that from this moment forward, Nemtori will serve in the royal household, as personal servant and attendant to our honored First Minister Promdjuk."

Not a murmur this time, but a short shock of sound—a combination of sharp inbreaths and stifled oaths, followed by sustained muttering. Oreg, in a manner clearly planned beforehand, stepped another step forward, and the soldiers standing around the perimeter of the room snapped to attention and beat their spear-butts on the floor.

Zilumek made a grand gesture with his arms. "Let there now be jubilee!" he called out. It was the traditional end of the coronation. Horns and drums burst into joyful noise. A few strong voices, primed for the moment, rose in a song of celebration, and others quickly joined in. Almond performed a reverence and returned to veir parents, who stood open-mouthed.

Then whatever affronted sensibilities there might still have been among those gathered were submerged, at least for the time being, in the raucous tumult of festivity.

Chapter 54

ALMOND PREPARED for veir first meeting with Promdjuk with less than veir usual aplomb. Vo was not accustomed to feeling nervous, and after trying first one wrap, then another, then the first again, vo gave vent to a rare outburst of frustration, throwing down the garment vo held. Loshi, busy but watching, said quietly, "Nemtori, dear one, don't fret. It doesn't matter what you wear. All will be well." Almond gave veir mother a grateful glance and then hurried to veir appointment.

Promdjuk had taken up residence in Nak's old quarters, for as long as any record had been kept the chambers of the First Minister. Almond stopped outside the door and anxiously checked veir clothes one more time. Vo knocked. "Come in," said the voice inside. Almond entered.

The room lay in some disarray; its new occupant was still taking ownership. Nak's few remaining trappings lay jumbled in a corner. New furniture had been brought, but not yet arranged.

"Nemtori, welcome," the looming old man said, in his halting Nezel. "Please to sit." Almond obeyed, trying by quick obedience to show that vo received the use of veir native tongue as a mark of respect. The elder lowered himself carefully onto his low pallet, his knees poking up at awkward angles. "I am old," he said, switching to his own language, "and my time in the tunnels has taken its toll."

"Aye, Ruler."

"You have been sent to serve me."

"Aye, Ruler."

"I am glad. Already in our short time together you have aided me, and I have also witnessed the care you take of the others around you."

Almond felt veir face warm at this unexpected compliment. "Thank you, Ruler."

"So, part of your duties will be to help me as I need. For example, I can only with difficulty stand up from this pallet alone."

Almond, taking this for an order, scrambled to help him rise. Promdjuk held up a hand. "In due time," he said. "I thank you." Abashed, Almond sat down again.

"There are other ways I may need your help," Promdjuk went on. "Not all of them pleasant."

Almond opened veir mouth, then closed it again. A sudden love for this stately old human infused veir heart. "Ruler," vo said. "I am honored to serve. And I care little about . . . I am not disturbed by . . . things of the body."

"It is well. But, Nemtori, helping me through my days is only part of your work, and not the most important part."

Almond waited.

"In the last few days, I have had words with my friend Sarvi, who lowered me my baskets all those years. And Sarvi has told me that you, Nemtori, have certain talents."

"Ruler?"

"Sarvi said, 'Young Almond excels at seeing and hearing. Vo finds things out.'"

Almond looked at the floor.

"And, said I, it is well. For the nub and kernel of the work of the First Minister is to know all that passes in the fortress, and to know as much as possible the minds and hearts of those who live there, so that harmony may be maintained."

Almond's face clouded. Vo opened veir mouth, hesitated, and closed it again.

"Speak your mind, Nemtori," Promdjuk said. "This I shall always expect of you."

"Ruler . . . it is true I know some secret places. And sometimes I . . . take pleasure . . . in seeing and hearing somewhat of the business of the fortress from them. But . . ."

"But what?"

Almond studied the face before ven. It was difficult to read. Much care and suffering, this old man had endured, and yet he seemed kind. Also, though, there was a hardness there. Was it strength to persevere, only? Or did it also include the will to control and dominate? Did he have the capacity for cruelty? "Ruler," Almond said, "it was only ever for my own amusement. And though I sometimes shared some of what I learned with certain of my own people, I was never sent expressly to spy."

"I see." Promdjuk ran one of his huge hands over his face. "Nor do I send you expressly to spy. Let us say only, that as far as my authority extends, you enjoy free access to all this fortress, leaving aside only the royal apartments. And if, in the course of your duties, in carrying out the errands I will give to you, you should happen to see or hear aught that it seems to you that a First Minister might find useful to know for the better managing of this place and the well-being of all within it, it would not be amiss for you to convey such information to me, in moments when we are alone."

The two humans, young and old, of different races, of different histories and statures in the place they inhabited, looked long into each other's eyes. Wary though Almond was, vo could find in the old man's expression no malice, no lust for power; only the same curiosity about and concern for the welfare of other humans that vo felt veirself—the same care for all who worked and played and ate and slept and loved and worshiped and rejoiced and suffered and died in the Desert Fortress.

"Aye, Ruler," Almond said at last. "It shall be as you command."

The old man smiled. "Well, then," he said. "It is very well. And now, if you will be so kind, I require your assistance to stand up from this pallet."

Chapter 55

PROMDJUK PROVED to be a demanding but fair task-master. Almond was kept busy helping him tend to the needs of his body, broken in some ways beyond healing by his long time in the dark places under the castle. The rest of the time vo was sent running errands and messages all over the citadel. The fortress bustled and steamed and clanged with eager new energy, sometimes chaotic but almost always cheerful, as the truth of recent developments settled deeper into its inhabitants' minds, and the people begin to trust the rule of their new monarch.

The slow turn of the seasons could be felt as a changed flavor of the air, though the heat still mounted and oppressed in the afternoon, and for a span each day the fortress drowsed in a haze of insect noise and sunglare. On the ninth day of veir new service, Almond was sent during this somnolent time to bear a message to the priestess of the temple of the Innumerable. Moving through the bake and dust, Almond enjoyed the sensation of being the only one stirring.

On soundless feet vo floated around one bend and another, approaching the archway that led into a secret little side garden, and then on into the tessellated wonder of the temple. The habit of stealth slowed veir footsteps as vo approached the last corner. Vo stood still a moment and practiced silent breathing before easing veir eyes past the edge of the wall. The green grotto was not empty, as vo had expected. Oreg was there. Almond suppressed the impulse to jerk back out of sight.

The huge captain of the guards sat on a stone bench, ungainly in his bulk, and it took Almond another moment to perceive that someone else was there as well. At first Almond could not see who the other was, but after a moment the further figure shifted, bringing his face into view, and Almond saw that it was Eo, only lately released from the healer's chambers. The last blow issued by Kretsipom in the final few seconds of his life had almost killed the young musician. Almost, but not quite; and now, it seemed, he was on the mend.

From where Almond watched, vo could see only a sliver of Oreg's face, but vo was able clearly to discern that the two sat close together on the bench, leaning their heads toward each other, speaking words too quiet for their clandestine watcher to hear. Presently Almond saw a slim hand reach around and hold the heavy jaw of the Captain of the Guards for a moment in a tender caress.

Heart wrung by emotions vo would have struggled to name, Almond silently withdrew. This was one secret that vo would never share with Promdjuk or any other.

***

Toward sunset on the same day, Almond sat under a lemon tree in the orchard, veir back against its trunk. Sarvi, coming to inspect the growing fruit, found ven there.

"Well now, little nut."

Almond did not reply. Sarvi took a second look at veir young friend's face, and said, "Does something trouble you?"

Almond glanced up, then away. Absently, veir fingers felt into the secret pocket and brought out a brown seedpod to work. Sarvi set aside veir basket and sat down in the shade, close but not touching, and waited.

At last Almond turned back. Vo struggled to find words. "Cerach. I . . . I could not love him. Not in the way he wanted. I could not be . . . the girl he wanted to love."

Sarvi reached out a hand and briefly pressed Almond's shoulder.

"If I could have . . . but I couldn't. I have to be who I am."

Another shoulder press, but still no words from the patient listener.

Almond's face took on a wretched expression. "I know to the bottom of my soul that I made the right choice at Naming—that, at least, I feel completely sure about—but I'm afraid that . . . I must be broken, somehow, because I have never felt . . . my heart has never felt . . . Sarvi, is there something wrong with my heart?" During this outburst, Almond had broken open the tree egg. Veir fingers sought another.

Sarvi sat silent. Almond swiped at a wet eye-corner. Sarvi said, "Nemtori, there is nothing wrong with your heart. You are young. The sweet ache may well come in time." Vo paused. "And yes, it sometimes leads to more trouble than joy, but still, it is so very sweet."

Tough old Sarvi spoke with feeling, and Almond found veirself jostled out of veir misery by quick curiosity. Had Sarvi felt love? Almond had always assumed that veir elder's proud aloofness had been and would be lifelong, eternal. Vo opened veir mouth to ask, but Sarvi's eye's glinted, anticipating and forbidding the question. The moment struck Almond suddenly as comical, and vo laughed a little. Sarvi's mouth twitched. "Pert one."

"Yes, Sarvi."

"Nemtori, you may yet feel the ache, or you may not. All are good paths." The orchard-keeper stared off over the wall. The sky was darkening slowly toward night. After a long silence, Almond shifted as if to rise, but stopped again when Sarvi said, "Nemtori."

"Yes, Sarvi?"

The elder gazed down at veir fingers, which toyed with a fallen twig. "Listen, Nemtori. I have been thinking. It was a noble thing our new young lord did, bringing you into service under old Promdjuk. Noble and canny. A bold move hard for any to resist, with him in the new flush of his power."

"Yes, Sarvi," Almond murmured.

"But—and I think you must have thought of this too—it cannot last." Sarvi glanced to see Almond's nod. "Promdjuk is not well and cannot live long. Certainly not as long as you will, with all your life still in front of you." The orcharder's face moved in an unusual way, and Almond wondered if vo could have seen right. Was it a touch of bashfulness vo had just glimpsed? Sarvi went on: "So what I thought was, between times, when your other duties permit, perhaps you could come here, and I could teach you the care of these trees." Sarvi swallowed and continued more quietly. "I, too, come to the end of my years," vo said. "And I fear for my trees after I am gone, if no one knows their ways. They live longer than we do. Their slow memory, breathing through the seasons, watches us flicker and pass."

When Almond answered, veir voice was full of tenderness. "Yes, Sarvi. With all my heart. I would learn the ways of the trees."

"Good," Sarvi said, a touch of roughness in veir voice. "Let it be so."

As dusk continued to deepen, the two sat on in pensive silence. At length Almond made a small sound of distress.

"What is it?" Sarvi said. "Does something else trouble you?"

"Yes, Sarvi. I would learn the care of the trees, but there is something my mother said, after Cerach went away. She said that perhaps in time we, the rest of the family, might follow. She said we might try to go back closer to Nezel, whether the rebels have won or no."

"That does not surprise me," Sarvi answered quietly. "I have sometimes thought the same myself." Vo reached up and tenderly caressed a low-hanging lemon leaf. "And though it would pain my heart deeply to leave these trees with no one who knows their care, yet, if such a journey was to be made, I would want to go." Vo caught and held Nemtori's gaze.

"Keep me in your counsels," vo said. "If a decision is made, I want to know."

"Yes, Sarvi," Almond said. "I will tell my mother. It will be so."

"That is good." Sarvi rubbed the back of veir neck, sighed, and began to struggle to veir feet. Almond shifted close to offer a shoulder to grip. "In the meantime," the orchard-keeper said, "By valor and luck, we have escaped a great evil. We serve, but the one we serve seems just and kind. We have our Street of Jewels and the community it holds. We have honest work for our hands to do. And though we are far from home, brave ones from among us fight still for us, and we may yet hope to someday return to our own land." Standing now, Sarvi quoted an old Nezel benediction: "May the Three watch over us and guide us truly on the paths we walk."

Almond, also risen now, found no words to say. Movement overhead caught veir eye. A great blue heron, neck curled back on itself, long stick legs jutting out behind, glided by on stiffly cupped wings, heading it seemed for the green bend of the river. As Sarvi moved off between the rows of trees in the direction of the servants' gate, on veir way back to the Street of Jewels for the evening meal, Almond lingered to track the bird's flight. The heron dropped down out of view in front of the moon, which was just rising above the ridgeline of the hills. The crescent of its face was partially obscured by a soft bar of cloud—the first cloud to appear in this particular bowl of the heavens since summer had begun.

Gazing at the mist-blurred face of the moon, Nemtori felt a bone-deep loosening in veir body. Vo rolled veir head on veir neck, veir shoulders in veir sockets, listening to the crackle of the release of tensions long-held. Vo heaved a profound sigh. "We serve," Sarvi had said, and it was true—but, Almond suddenly realized, it didn't matter. "With my feet on the Way," vo murmured to veirself, "no matter what the circumstances of my life, I will always be a dancer of the Dance. No matter what the circumstances of my life, I will always be free."

Vo closed veir eyes reverently and, in veir mind, uttered a silent prayer of thanksgiving to Meb Netál and to the Three. Then vo turned to follow Sarvi, walking on silent, purposeful feet, heading home.

ABOUT THE AUTHOR

Lisa Bunker writes rainbow novels for young readers. Veir previous works include *Felix Yz* (2017) and *Zenobia July* (2019). Vo has made homes in New Mexico, the LA area, Seattle, the Florida panhandle, Maine, and New Hampshire. Vo now lives in Sacramento, California, with veir spouse Dawn, an expert on anxiety in children and an author in her own right. Between them, they have three grown children. Lisa is a longtime trans/enby activist, and from 2018 to 2022 vo represented the town of Exeter in the New Hampshire House of Representatives. Veir interests include chess, birding, choral singing, and playing bass and piano.

www.lisabunker.net

www.ingramcontent.com/pod-product-compliance
Lightning Source LLC
Chambersburg PA
CBHW020808190726
48285CB00006B/2200